LO

by the same author

CURFEW AND OTHER STORIES

SEAN O'REILLY

Love and Sleep
A Romance

ff

faber and faber

First published in 2002
by Faber and Faber Limited
3 Queen Square London WC1N 3AU

Typeset by Faber and Faber Limited
Printed in England by Clays Ltd, St Ives plc

The text contains a quotation from *News for the Delphic Oracle*
by William Butler Yeats.

The author would like to acknowledge the receipt of a bursary from
the Arts Council of Ireland, An Chomhairle Ealaíon, to help in the
completion of this book.

A CIP record for this book is available from the British Library

ISBN 0–571–20545–3

2 4 6 8 10 9 7 5 3 1

for Smoke-Ring

He is androgyne because he comes from an androgyne father, and he never sleeps because he comes from one who is sleepless. Yet love and sleep are his masters.

The Hermetica (translated by Brian P. Copenhaver)

Prologue

At a party, an overcrowded room, after a funeral – I didn't know the man they had left in the side of the hill above the city of Derry. Lorna is standing near me, listening to a woman in a black headscarf whose face seems to grow more and more salacious. Lorna is drunk; I am drunk, full of vindictive excitement.

I must have been asleep for days. The last light is making a sordid lair of the room; people are constantly glancing towards the small window and the cramped passage of the ominous clouds over the rooftops and the streets and the back lanes. The laughter has ceased for the moment. I have to fight off a nagging urge to throw my glass at the nearest wall. Lorna is staring at me mournfully out of the dusk, self-absorbed, unanswerable, the flame of a candle swaying near her, glistening sickly on the black stones hanging from her ears. I can't bear to look at her for a second longer.

A woman with a long white neck pushes past me; I grab her by the shoulder and turn her around to face me. I can see straight away that she doesn't recognize me. I had met her for the first time a few hours earlier in the pub.

Is there anything more to drink? I ask, gloating on the hostility in her eyes.

You've had enough, she sneers at me with a bored sigh.

I find myself searching her eyes for some trace of the moment when she discovered her lover lying under the bed, face up, his hands joined, where he had chosen to die. A smile grows across my mouth.

Do you find something amusing?

Everywhere I look, I tell her, still smirking. Even under the bed.

They were right about you, she says and stretches her neck.

I think I'm going to go mad in here, I whisper to her. Do you want to go out for some air?

Over her shoulder, Lorna continues to watch me, a dreary debt in her eyes. I am suffocated by shame at the sight of her – the memory of her naked body, her clumsiness, her sincerity, her cold breasts.

I want to beg the white-throated women to save me, to help me escape, but I know I would be unable to keep her attention.

He'll miss that neck, I tell her and steal a kiss of it.

She didn't flinch: You're not worth slapping.

That morning, I had woken up and gone straight out into the street where I ran into Danny, who was on his way to find me. He was wearing a suit and tie. I was supposed to be with Lorna at the cemetery, he reminded me. When he saw the look of reluctance on my face, he immediately lost his temper.

She's standing up there on her own, he pointed up the street.

It's a funeral. Everybody is, I said. I've never even met the man anyway, Danny.

She was waiting for you at the cemetery. You told her you'd go with her. She's enough on her plate.

Has she? I couldn't help laughing at this show of solidarity with her.

She knew him, Danny said firmly, as though it was the bottom line. For a moment he seemed embarrassed by the portentous tone in his voice. He went on more carefully: You said you'd be there. She's known him for years.

So have you.

His face went blank; he shook his head.

She's in her element. Suicide and tragedy. Doom and wind and graves. She loves it. She's jealous.

Danny dropped his beleaguered gaze. He stared at the ground between us as though it sickened him. His meekness sometimes made me afraid of him, and of that half-hung city.

Are you coming or not? he said quietly then, to my relief. She needs a bit of support today. Somebody's died, that's all.

We went to the Lesson and started drinking. Danny told a group of us a story about Jim, the dead man. He put on voices and mimed a variety of expressions: I had never heard him tell a story with any conviction before. He became flushed and exhilarated – everyone seemed saddened by his fervour. A rotted déjà vu greeted me on all sides. I went outside to clear my head. It was a Sunday and the street was empty. A man was whistling merrily to himself in the darkened arch of one of the old city gates, looking down at the Bogside where there was no sign of anyone. Going past the new shopping centre a gang of dressed-up teenagers were gathered outside a music shop, passing around a joint. I thought of Valeria and her favourite café in a crowded shopping centre in Rome where we always argued, where she would mix sachets of sugar into her tears on the table. I sniffed at my clothes but the sweet wheaten smell of her was gone.

Back in the pub, someone introduced me to the dead man's girlfriend with her staggering white neck. Holding her hand, I talked to her giddily about whatever came into my head. It was a struggle not to pull on her hand suddenly and rub her knuckles against my groin. Then I told her what I wanted to do; she looked at me as though I was overstating the obvious (I thought maybe she had taken a sedative).

Lorna was avoiding me. Later, in the back yard of the house, the dead man's clothes were set on fire as they hung on the line – underwear, socks, a T-shirt from Morocco and faded oriental pyjamas. It was raining, and dark. Above the city a helicopter was taunting a silent street. The girlfriend began to cry, flailing and kicking at whoever came near her, twisting her long neck in the centre of the crowd as though she were dancing with the flames. I saw Lorna looking down at this scene from the lighted window.

. . . She is sitting next to me on the floor of the dead man's house, her knees up under a long dark skirt, and there's black soldier's boots. She knows I don't want her anywhere near me. Feigning boredom, she is picking at the knotted muslin around her palm; the clumsily tied bandage suits her. She wants to remind me of what I did to her; or worse, she is tenderly revisiting the moment a few hours before when I tried to take the glass out of her hands to refill my own. She wouldn't let go. I squeezed her thick hands together until the glass shattered and the red wine jumped comically into the air between us. As they led her out of the room, she looked back at me without anger or surprise, a black strand of hair stuck to the wine on her cheek. I hated her; she seemed almost compliant, and proud, like she knew this had been coming.

All I feel is angry, she says to me on the floor. Not anger about guilt or him going but anger that . . . he was right. What he said was right. I never wanted to believe him. He knew himself. He could see what was going to happen.

He killed himself, I reminded her.

So?

He didn't have to.

You don't believe that.

I was revolted by her conviction that she knew me. I fought to control myself.

You would have liked him, she went on. He'd travelled a lot but he was always coming back. When he was really down, he used to be convinced that he'd arrive back one day and the whole city would be deserted. He wanted to write something as well.

What does that mean? As well?

She didn't answer me. She was glaring at the people around the fireplace.

Look at them. They don't give a damn about anyone but themselves.

Are you any different?

She doesn't answer this either.

They're enjoying themselves, I go on in the same spiteful way. Everybody except you.

You only pretend to enjoy yourself, she says as she takes my hand. You try to . . . but you just end up making a mockery of it.

I'm only here because Danny caught me on the street. Do you think I wanted to be here? I don't care who he was.

Can't I stroke your hand? she whines and gives me a sarcastic smile.

I have to close my eyes to control my revulsion.

None of this would have been unknown to her. I spent time with her because I couldn't bear my own loneliness. Through me she sought to confirm some depressing hypothesis to herself. During the few deranged months we knew each other, I lived at the extreme edge of myself; she made me feel that there was nothing to stop me going even further. She fascinated and appalled me because I didn't want her – because it was impossible to want her. Lorna understood this without enthusiasm. Her lugubrious demeanour was ham-fisted and often absurd.

You're avoiding me, she says mawkishly. Talk to me. Tell me about something. You've stopped talking to me.

You sound almost pleased, I turn to her, my teeth jammed together to prevent me shouting. Aren't you? To shut me up. That's what you want.

Slowly, she shakes her head and smiles at me patronizingly. Why are you so angry at me? She tries to be soothing, but manages only to make me feel that she is about to burst out laughing.

Desperate for a way out of this, I say: I'm drunk . . . And you're drunk too.

You don't talk to me any more, she says then. Lorna would never admit to being drunk.

Before I can speak, she says in a different tone of voice, sulking: It's a waste of time anyway, I suppose. People talk far too much. You know the old Jews? When they had a dream, they wouldn't tell anybody, until they found the right person they could trust. Not because it was private but because it was dangerous to. The first time you told the dream, then that became what the dream meant, how you understood it. One chance only. You could get it wrong. And it might be an important message. So you had to find the right person. Not run around shouting it to all and sundry. We should all shut up. Go on strike. You have art strikes, so we can have dream strikes, love strikes, God strikes, sex strikes . . .

She starts laughing now, her coarse, straining, barren wheeze. In front of the fireplace, a few people are listening gravely to an older bearded man who I have seen around the pubs, always with a girl or two, calling for his drinks in Gaelic. Just then, the dead man's girlfriend comes into the room with Danny, her arm around his waist. She refuses Danny's suggestion to talk to us and leads him towards the fireplace.

I've been having the dream again, Lorna announces, tightening her grip on my hand, but then: No, I'm not going to talk about it any more.

She is waiting for me to ask her to tell me more.

Jim never trusted her an inch, I hear Lorna announce after a while, glaring at the group around the fireplace. He told me that a few times.

This makes me laugh ruefully because Lorna rarely allowed herself to dislike people.

Here's a question then, she says to distract us from the ones around the fireplace. You can only answer yes or no. And you are not allowed to discuss your answer. Ever.

At this point, I lose control over myself. I start shouting at her: That's not a question. That's a gun . . . That's a gun jammed into your mouth. The world's not like that. We're not responsible, Lorna. You're trying to kill it. And me as well. Strikes and guns. You have a nightmare and now the world's got to pay for it . . . You're poison. You're killing everything. It's just a dream.

I was on my feet now, roaring my head off at her. I went on like this, without understanding much of what I was saying.

Danny turned up at my side; I was pointing at Lorna and shouting at Danny. Eventually he coaxed me into another room with him; there was music and people dancing which helped me settle down. Lorna merely gaped up at me with that same exasperating sorrow in her big eyes – she was like a child pretending to be sorry, but the reason for her charade was beyond my comprehension.

She found me in a bedroom much later in the night. I woke up, soaked in sweat, and saw a misshapen figure in the cold brightness of the doorway. For an instant only, I was terrified: the blood seemed to dry up and turn to dust in my veins. I remembered with horror that I was sleeping in the house of a man who had gone into the ground only a few hours earlier. The earth was pressing around him, sniffing him, blowing on him. I could smell the stewed warmth of flesh from the grieving apparition in the doorway. To my own bewilderment, I wasn't able to move because my hand was still jammed up between the legs of a girl lying next to me.

I'm going, Lorna said, attempting to sound natural.

What the hell do you think you're saying? I had no idea what I meant by this.

Again, she ignored me.

Will I close the door? This sham of gentleness enraged me.

Sweet dreams, I shouted after her. Sweet dreams. I tried to laugh.

This is not a waning.
The twilight groans . . . and drapes the streets in a filthy caul. This is the fledgling time. The world is damp yet and unwashed.

A dismal immanence seeps out of the sky. At this hour I am unable to summon the courage to be afraid of death (I find it disgusting but I accept that death is no better than I deserve). Don't misunderstand me: I am not being humble.

This morning I saw her kneeling at the corner in the snow.

She was wearing her long black coat. A tram passed along the street and the driver rang the bell. Then everyone on the tram jumped up and started banging on the windows at her with their gloved hands, waving and shouting; some of them were weeping with joy. It was the first time she has appeared outside of my dreams.

I thought I was going mad back then in Derry – insolently, I didn't even try to prevent myself. I had forgotten Lorna until a few weeks ago when the letter from Danny arrived. It is nearly three years since I last saw him; he started shouting at me in the pub, accusing me of not looking after her and not believing her and then he fell on the floor, scratching with his hands at the boards like he was digging for something. I left Derry again before the hangover of that night had faded.

In the letter he tells me he has just got out of a mental hospital where he spent almost a year. He mentions Lorna only at the very end: Do you think we could have done anything to stop her? On his first morning out, he went to visit her grave and made a rubbing of the inscription on the stone (he started doing this kind of thing while in hospital, tracing the surfaces of tables and floors to occupy his time, people's hands, windows and mirrors). Lorna's father now lies on top of her; Danny says he'll send me on the rubbing if I want it. He has a job behind the bar of a new pub, the biggest so far, with four floors, in the post-past city, as he jokingly describes it. He sells the socialist papers every Saturday outside one of the new shopping centres.

I read the letter to the man in the café I talk to in the mornings. He wears a thin red handkerchief tied around his neck to hide his hunting scars. When I was finished, he tore the letter into pieces and dropped them into my drink.

That's my advice, he said. Drink it.

Day after day the sky is the same – like a crisp blue flame. She steps into my dreams out of some dark corner and bows to me politely, with one raised sceptical eyebrow, but she keeps herself at a distance as though she intends only to observe. She follows me wherever I go. So I have decided to write about her, about the brief time I knew her in Derry. She will see that I lack any urge to confess – I have nothing to tell her, no dream for her ears alone. I don't need company. Or forgiveness, or any cure at knife-point.

Maybe then she will go away, like a beggar who squirms in disgust at your heartfelt apologies for having nothing to spare.

PART ONE

Martina sat on the arm of the sofa trying to make conversation. She wanted to know about my travels, as she called them. I hadn't taken off my coat; I was tired out and nervous about my own listlessness. My rucksack steamed in the corner of the room like an old dog let in out of the rain. The television flashed in spasms by the patio doors.

We went to London last summer, she said, delighted with herself for finding something that would certainly interest me. Michael didn't like it but I loved it. You know, you go over there and see so many different kinds of people and you wonder why the wee crowd of us over here can't just get on with things. Don't you think? India though; that's where I'd love to go. You been there as well, I suppose?

I shook my head. Her gaze flitted uneasily from the door to me in the chair. Ever since I had first met her, my sister-in-law had always talked as though the briefest pause or silence threatened to destroy the reason she was sitting there with you. Her hair was cut shorter, tied back with a child's velvet ribbon, but she had lost the delicacy about her face.

I've always had this feeling that I'll get there one day, she went on, giving me a sly wink. Since I was no height. When I met your Michael, I remember, he promised he would take me. Then he promised again we would go for the honeymoon. I'm worse for believing him. Can you see your Michael in India? Incense and palaces, no glass in the windows, steamy gardens . . . You know there's a touch of the exotic in me, I think . . . She laughed dreamily. You never know what's going to happen but, do you? There's your brother out in the kitchen and our Louise up the stairs . . . Give him a bit of time, Niall, will you?

I should go on, I managed to say, and suddenly Valeria

appeared with violent clarity in front of me: breathless, dazed, the water pouring over her strong bare shoulders, her perfect teeth, straight out of the sea. The smell of Rome in my clothes filled me with loneliness. I had been travelling for two days. Valeria was sleeping when I left, her brown, fresh-baked skin unmarked by the tears of the night before, and I walked across the lopsided courtyard . . . and on to the train station where a group of young soldiers sat in a circle playing cards and an old man in a dress and a shawl was sharpening the end of a stick with a penknife, whistling a song Valeria used to sing when she was happy, after she had eaten or put on a dress.

Sure you've just got here, Martina forced a laugh. You're only in the door.

It'd be easier probably.

Sit where you are, she said, losing her patience with me. What do you expect, Niall? He's angry at you. I've been married to him long enough to know him. Give him a chance. You can't just show up and not expect some kind of . . . Can you?

I nodded my acquiescence. I don't know where I am, Martina. I don't even think I actually intended to come back here.

You're here now, she said impatiently.

All I wanted was sleep. With tears of self-pity in my eyes, I stared at the glass of stout Martina had brought in for me. Like a man who can't believe in the reality of what he has just done – I felt sickened by a sense of powerlessness as I tried to remember waiting for the train in Rome and then Milan, and if I had actually told myself that the time had come and I was making my way back to Derry. I must have been in a state of shock. There was a young girl on the night train through France, a teenager, green-eyed, shaking under the cloying duress of her own sensuality, who followed me out into the corridor . . .

The air in the room was unsettled when I came back to myself. Martina was standing in front of the television,

4

staring at the silent screen; I had the impression that my brother had just gone out of the room without shutting the door.

Was I asleep?

Martina turned towards me and her face was pale and angry. She scowled at me defiantly, as though she was forcing me to witness the confusion and pain my return had caused. Just as I thought I couldn't take any more, her eyes closed for a second . . . She sighed heavily: What am I supposed to do, Niall? Tell me that. Do you know what I was just thinking about? The morning you left. Do you remember it?

Laughing hysterically, I held up the glass of stout, which was almost empty, but I couldn't find the words to explain that I was sure I hadn't drunk any. Martina was too engrossed in her own memories to take much notice of my ridiculous behaviour. She was remembering the bus in the morning fog, the driver with the tattoos, an alarm from across the river, shivering, the last time she had seen me.

. . . We all laughed when that old woman sat in next to you. The look on your face. You were so embarrassed. Your mother singing. And your father stayed sat in the car with all the windows steamed up. He was a cold man, we all know that. He couldn't help it. The men of his time were all like that. Think what they lived through – the forties and fifties in Northern Ireland; they were treated worse than animals. And then you going off to university. How can they make sense of changes like that, Niall? You should think about it.

It's got nothing to do with the past, I found myself saying, more to stop myself from laughing than anything else.

What's it got to do with, then?

There was nothing to come back for.

God forgive you. These are your own people.

I'll decide who my own people are, I said bombastically, or if I even want a people.

I put down the glass and stood up.

I'm going to head on, I said.

You can't just run away from it, Niall. The two of youse are just the same. Sit there for me, will you? For me? OK?

There's no point, I said, as a wave of nausea passed through me. Sweat broke out all over my face; I thought I was going to faint.

Martina threw herself on to the sofa and covered her face with a cushion. I wanted to speak but was afraid I was going to vomit. The television splattered coloured shadows violently across the walls of the room.

I'm just a waste, I said, collapsing into the chair again.

You were missed, you know, Martina began to say, looking at the velvet cushion she was holding out before her, turning it over, untangling the golden lace tassels. Your father's own funeral . . . then our wedding . . . then your mother's stroke. People ask themselves why. They blame themselves. Deep down under the anger they blame themselves. They want to know what they've done. A father dies and a son doesn't come to the funeral . . . so what are people supposed to think?

She looked across at me, raising the eyebrows on her thickening face, waiting for me to say something to help her understand, some new excuse she could tell my brother which would make him forgive me.

I didn't want to, I told her. These were the cruellest words I could think of.

Martina nodded, biting her bottom lip.

It's that simple, she said in an effort to control herself. I thought so.

The telephone rang and we listened to my brother's voice in the hall. His wife said quietly to me: For my sake, Niall, and our Louise up the stairs, please try and make peace with him.

It took all my concentration to hold in the vomit until my brother had finished on the phone. I went in and lay down on the bathroom floor, exhausted and delirious – hordes of children were rushing towards me from all sides; they were naked and painted, I could hear their voices getting nearer, and I saw myself running in terror through the streets and into the forest as they pursued me.

My brother was waiting outside the bathroom door for me.

In spite of all my efforts, I couldn't manage to look him in the eye.

Take it easy on me, I implored him. I'm not feeling well.

Neither am I. At the sight of you, he said with unnatural slowness. Do you understand me? This is my house. And you're not welcome. You're here because that Martina wants you to be. Not me.

I'll go.

Just don't even bother speaking to me. You've a couple of days. A week at the most. I take it you're only gracing us with a wee visit anyway. Then I want to see the back of you. Do you hear me? And one wrong word, one bad look, especially to our Louise, and you won't know what hit you. Clear? Nobody gives a damn about whatever nonsense has sent you running back here. Do you hear me?

I kept myself from speaking; I could feel him studying me with contempt. It was asking too much of him to expect him to hit me.

2

One afternoon I went for a walk around the city centre. I had nothing else to do. This was in the first few days of those frantic months when I tried to return, if that was what I was doing, to the queasy, humble streets between the hills and the river. The river there was always too big and contented for the place, too full of itself.

The first face that recognized me – it was only the bloated, uninterested face of someone I had known at school, out shopping with a woman and two young children – made me reel with shame. A few steps later another face looked at me twice and I was sure some comment was passed . . . I veered off into a quieter street and leaned against a wall, then felt too conspicuous. There was nowhere to go to escape from people who knew my name, those wry, adamant eyes. I couldn't understand why I felt so humiliated and petrified merely being seen on the street. There was a small pub opposite; although I remembered it was an old man's place, I was too scared to enter. *Occhi . . . occhi . . .* I kept repeating to myself in Italian, fistfuls of *occhi . . .*

A few girls appeared at the top of the cobbled street. As they came nearer, laughing among themselves, I leaned back against the wall and tried to appear at my ease, as though waiting for somebody to come out of the pub or the bookie's further along. No matter what I did to appear unremarkable, they sensed my embarrassment and their laughter stopped. I couldn't lift my eyes from the ground. My face, I knew, was bright red. The girls slowed down as though afraid to pass me. Unable to bear any more of this, I bolted across the street like a frightened animal and at the last minute, to my relief, spotted a narrow flight of steps.

I was up on the old walls of the city, looking out over the newly scrubbed Bogside with its painted verandas, satellite dishes and hidden alleyways. The main streets were tidy and empty. On the side of a block of flats there was a gigantic mural of a boy in a gas mask, calmly waiting, in the smoke and mayhem of the riot, for the right moment to let fly with his petrol bomb. A wind was blowing up towards me but nothing moved.

I reminded myself that this was city where I was born and grew up; I had no reason to sneak around as though I was afraid of being caught. Why should I be ashamed and nauseous? What had I done? In this frame of mind, I decided to walk around the circumference of the old battlements, telling myself that it would be good for me in some way. The polished cannons with their gullets cemented shut pointed out over a crowd gathered in the Guildhall Square. About fifty people, some with placards, stood around a low stage, while a few others accosted passers-by with leaflets and slogans. There was a lorry parked at the side of the stage loaded with balloons. A man was shouting into a microphone, advocating a strike at a local factory; I detested him immediately. No matter how he tried to employ the gestures of a man who is

8

outraged at injustice, he couldn't conceal his caution and meanness.

Next, a young worker took over the hailer. I had come down the steps to join the crowd by that stage, driven along by aversion. The speaker had retreated into the background; he clapped and punched the air at the wrong moment. Someone spoke to me then and I turned round in confusion.

Are you supporting the strike? a woman had asked me. I saw a horseshoe-shaped frown and heaped black hair. Across her arm, tidily arranged like serviettes, she was carrying a pile of socialist newspapers. I must have been staring hard at them.

Do you want a paper?

I tried to look at her again but it was as if I was facing into the wind. I had the impression of white stains under dark eyes, a large and flaccid face. She was wearing a faded denim jacket.

Are you in support of the strike? she asked again more slowly. She said later that she wondered if I was on drugs. Behind her, I noticed two girls who were laughing and holding on to one another's waist as they tried to light a cigarette in the wind.

Are you all right? the woman was curious to know, and stroked the newspapers across her arm.

Who's the one at the mike?

The speaker was back at the front of the platform: The worker in Derry has no rights. The British government is handing out grants and subsidies to big businesses. You're fired on the spot if you stand up for your rights. No trouble-makers allowed. If we don't fight back and support these men, the big businesses will walk all over us. They'll disappear as soon as the grants dry up.

That's Emmet Martin, she leaned closer to me confidentially. This was bound to happen. They've no regard for the community here or anywhere else. They're only here because they get a cheap and obedient workforce. It's just bribery. They're turning the Derry people against each other. We just

9

have to keep it non-sectarian. The media are twisting everything. It's not in their interests. You have to ask yourself why you're standing here and what you're going to do about it? You –

Her tirade of slogans finished as suddenly as it had begun. I tried to laugh to see how she would react but she smiled back at me, confidently and unembarrassed. This was a woman who believed it was necessary to confront a stranger on the street with her own opinions. She wore thick bracelets on both wrists, heavy earrings, a necklace of Celtic stones, a large bronze hair clip. Everything about her seemed big, overdone, excessive: the abundant hair, the shapeless clothes, the broad mouth, the hefty breasts under a black woollen jumper. Her eyes were dark: I can't remember the colour of her eyes.

With a pained expression, she went on: Emmet has done everything he can to show that this issue affects the workers on all sides. We have new members from all over. He goes over to the Protestant estates and knocks on doors, but he isn't allowed any protection. But it's starting to pay off. The socialist perspective is the best one. It's the only one left, she said, as though she had just thought of it. You're not from Derry then?

I must have appeared shocked.

It's just your accent. I thought it sounded strange, she said, trying to apologize. It's just me. I haven't a musical bone in my body.

I've been away for a while.

For a moment we both looked up at the sky where the grey had whitened and thinned and a seagull swerved at an impossible angle and cried once. A patch of blue opened above a man working on the clock spire. We listened to another burst of applause. Meanwhile, they were having trouble lifting an old man in white overalls up on to the stage. The speaker, uncomfortable with the delay, pretended to be oblivious by gesticulating intently to a woman at the front of the crowd.

If there's no such thing as truth, then there can't be any justice either, the paper-seller announced with touching sadness.

I started laughing.

Do you doubt it? she challenged me. Laughter isn't good enough any more.

You have beautiful hair.

I hadn't planned to say that. She was the first woman to speak to me other than Martina since I had arrived back. Startled, she opened her mouth to laugh but nothing came out. I began to make excuses for my behaviour: I'm sorry. I'm only back a couple of days. My head's in a state. I shouldn't have said it.

Too right you shouldn't. Her face was drained of colour with the shock.

But you'd rather listen to an old man anyway.

What?

Why do you want to listen to an old man? They all say the same thing – keep your head down and don't want too much.

How dare you? They've lived.

So have the dogs, I said nonsensically. And the worms.

You're the bloody worm, she said and took a threatening step towards me.

A man in the crowd heard this.

You all right there, Lorna?

She must have merely given him some look to say she could handle this pathetic headcase on her own. The man in the white overalls was talking too quietly into the mike. Lorna folded her arms and sized me up.

I began to mumble helplessly: I'm wandering around this city on my own. I don't know a being. Nobody. It's like I'm paranoid all the time . . . I follow the stray dogs for something to do. It's either that or sitting in the house – my brother's house. My tongue won't work right. And you look around and there's new shopping centres and new pubs and new car parks and scaffolding everywhere and I feel older than . . .

11

I lifted my eyes but I was alone. The crowd was applauding loudly. There were more people up on the stage. The speaker started the countdown and then the net was pulled away to release the balloons. Haltingly, a few of them rose into the air; some of the crowd ran towards the lorry to help them on their way.

3

A woman was pushing a pram up the hill towards me. The previous night I had spent in front of the television, drinking straight from a bottle of whiskey. In a fit of misery, I had called Valeria in Italy, but as soon as I heard her voice I put down the phone.

Two army Jeeps came slowly down the hill, a soldier standing up in each of them, camouflaged and bored, slouched over a gun. As they passed the woman with the pram who had stopped to catch her breath, she spat into their path. One of the soldiers stuck up a finger at her. My mother was in the building behind me: that's what I was doing there.

Leaning against the railings outside the home, I tried to imagine my mother, chain-smoking in a wheelchair, the long, raging attacks on imaginary visitors, her hats and scarves, pockets full of cutlery, winking lewdly at her own reflection. The nurses were tired of her violence; Martina told me all this. I had been there for nearly an hour, waiting without hope for a surge of courage, or humility, that would send me rushing in to see her. The idea that she might not know who I was left me indifferent.

Across the street, two men came out of a house and stood at the doorstep in silence. A flurry of seagulls and crows erupted into the low sky above the river – as though something momentous was finally about to break the surface of the water. I was hung-over and sick of my callous yearning for nothing at all. One of the men nodded in my direction, and then the other one with a moustache leaned out of his door for a better look at me. He spat on the ground. I had been there too long.

That evening I was in a bar with Danny. A few days earlier he had stepped up in front of me on the street and gripped my hands and laughed in admiration at the great craftiness that had brought us face to face again. Then, remembering he was dressed in a suit, he took me into a side street to confess that he was on his way to a job interview in a new hotel. I agreed to meet him later in the week, despite the feeling that we had nothing to say to each other.

There's me all envious thinking you'd be living it up, he said to me in the bar.

I was drunk after a few pints; even then, I was morose and made him nervous.

As a matter of fact, I was talking about you not so long ago. You mind Kieran Meehan? You must do. Well I ran into him one night when he was back and he was asking after you. He's over in the States making adverts or something, Danny laughed. Married and wains and the whole lot. Hard to believe, isn't it? When you think how off his head he was. Do you mind the time sure when he –

I don't give a damn about Kieran Meehan, I shouted unintentionally. I was convinced Danny was talking like this in order to avoid listening to me. Plainly dressed as always, his face thicker and pale, he struck me as annoyingly contented with himself – chastened into a kind of humility I considered to be both dubious and malevolent.

He took a slow drink from his pint: So what has you back?

I don't know, Danny. I was telling you; I was in Italy living with this girl and then it fell apart and I just left. I got on a train.

And ended up here, he said, throwing out his arms. And talking to the likes of me.

I didn't believe in this show of deprecation for a second. He pretended to hate the place while secretly knowing that he couldn't speak or breathe or hold his head up anywhere else. He had come to stay with me once in London, reluctantly in search of a job. I met him at the bus station, showed him around, and he slept on my bedroom floor. As each day went by, he grew quieter and paler, and found any excuse to stay indoors, usually in front of the television. After three weeks of this muteness, which was clearly unwilled and painful for him, he broke down in the kitchen one night while we were all eating, throwing glasses at the ceiling and shouting abuse at me. In the morning he woke me up, his coat on and his bag over his shoulder, and asked me if I knew the times of the buses back.

Sitting with him now in the pub, I asked him about that time simply because I knew it would embarrass him.

I just couldn't hack it, he said blithely. London's not for me. I gave Dublin a go as well, you know? It didn't work out just. He paused and, with a false sigh, said: We can't all be globe-trotting around the place. Some of us have to stay put. You make your own bed just.

That's how I feel here, Danny . . . the way you felt in London. Suffocated.

Sure it's just Derry, he laughed me off. A wee dot. A few pubs and too many shops. And too many corners. But sure what difference does it make anyway?

I keep thinking I've only come back because it was the worst thing I could have done. To humiliate myself. It scares the hell out of me just walking down the street.

Imagine having to do it every morning.

It's like I'm ashamed of being caught at something, Danny. You don't know whether you've failed by coming back or they're all smirking because they knew you'd fail. You know the way you dream of being caught naked at mass?

Danny gave me a confused, surprised look.

Suddenly I said: You know my Da died? You know I didn't turn up for it?

For some reason, I wanted to shock him now.

I didn't show up for it, I went on. I was in London and I got the message and didn't call. Our Michael won't even look at me. I told you: he wants me out.

14

There's bound to be a flat going somewhere. If you want, I'll ask around. You planning to stay for a while then or what?

I don't know. I'm broke, Danny.

Your Michael's all right. Anybody'll tell you that. A bit severe that's all, a bit hard to approach, but he's sound.

I'm not looking for him to forgive me, I said angrily.

There was a short silence. Danny played with the froth at the bottom of his glass.

So you've been in Italy as well, then?

I nodded, resigned to his distance from me.

He emptied the rest of his pint, turned to me and said carefully, searching for the right words: Maybe you're back for a reason. For a rest, that's all. Maybe you've had enough for a while. There's no shame in it. You're knackered. Things'll sort themselves out.

He laughed at himself: Listen to me telling you how you feel and I start to panic as soon as I cross the bridge. Just ignore anything I say. I haven't got a clue, that's all. How's the writing anyway? You still doing the stories?

It was me who laughed now. Danny tried to laugh along with me.

You given it up, then? I don't blame you. People only listen when it suits them. Do you think that's right or not?

He meant this question seriously. While he waited for me to answer, he started to whistle and tapped his long, trimmed fingernails against his glass. When he glanced up at me, I saw an unmistakable glimmer of mockery in his eyes. Stunned, I looked away: at that very moment, I spotted Lorna again.

Danny said he knew her but he refused to go over and speak to her.

She's one of them political ones, he informed me. Ones who don't think about anything else. Always in a gang, like they're plotting. There's only a handful of them but. They don't stand a chance. Listen to me; what would I know anyway?

But what's she like?

15

Danny shrugged: No different to anyone else. You see her around but she's always studying you hard, even if it's in the pub late on and you're drunk and having a laugh just. It's like you have to have something interesting to say to her all the time. She's always up the town handing out leaflets or newspapers. Socialist stuff.

Lorna was with a number of other people who gathered in a corner near the door. As she was taking off her long coat, she caught sight of Danny, who was at the bar; she smiled politely and Danny went over to her. Lorna seemed to do most of the talking. Danny put his hands in his pockets and nodded along. She seemed to grow more enthusiastic as she talked. Her hair was allowed to hang down that day in a ponytail. She had the air of someone who has spent the day outside, flushed and garrulous. Then she must have asked who he was with for they both turned to look in my direction.

She recognized me immediately, even in the shadows of the pub, but she gave nothing away to Danny, who was watching her expression, or to me, who stared bleakly back at her. When they finally turned their backs on me, however, I was overwhelmed by the paranoid idea that they were both talking about me, a doomed outsider, and I saw my naked body beaten and dumped in a ditch. I fled to the toilet where I stayed for a long time, trying to talk some sense into myself, and appalled at my frightened face in the rusting mirror: there was no mercy in the sight of myself any more.

Danny was at the bar with some other people after all this. He didn't introduce me.

After midnight we sat on the steps of a building by the river, drinking a bottle of American whiskey. It had started to rain – heavy, violent rain. Danny and I were at the gluttonous cusp of drunkenness. We regularly jumped to our feet, gasping and exuberant, choking on our words, pointing, as though we had glimpses of some fleeting, garish spectacle in the dark.

Danny's face was swollen with crying. He couldn't stop

talking, shouting, ranting: You don't have the right, you don't have the right. You can't afford to be in love. We've no money. Fiancée . . . Fiancée . . . Fiancée . . .

He was putting on a girl's voice, saying the word over and over again. We were both crying with rage and self-pity. It had taken him all night to tell me that he had been engaged recently; it had lasted until a couple of weeks before, when the girl gave him back the ring with the excuse that she couldn't marry a man who was destined to spend the rest of his life on the dole.

I wanted us to go round to her house without delay.

You'd be happy to eat peas out of a tin for ever, Danny squawked in the girl's voice. You don't want anything. You don't want to do anything. You don't want anything. You don't want anything out of life.

Pulling his hair, he jumped up and ran out into the rain.

You don't want what she wants, Danny, I shouted after him.

He was roaring like an animal somewhere out of sight. When he came back he was streaked with muck and holding a bunch of flowers he had torn up. He stood in front of me, drenched, stroking his face with the flowers.

It's my own fault, isn't it?

What are you talking about? I grabbed some of the flowers from him and began to eat them. I was furious; I wasn't in control of myself. A red light tilted and lurched on the river like an evil eye hypnotizing me. A siren was whining somewhere in the city.

We chewed the flowers and drank them down with the rest of the whiskey.

Eat the rich, I shouted out across the city.

I can't move, said Danny, showing me a mouth crammed with crushed petals. His teeth were blackened.

Watch out for the thorns, I said. The two of us found this hysterical.

Danny was sick first. He stood spread-eagled against the wall as though he was about to be searched. Despite vomiting,

17

we were still in the grip of an edgy exhilaration. Danny started to sing as we walked through the rain alongside the river, and the swaying red eye seemed to want more from us, winking from the depths of an obscene tranquillity. To my surprise, he knew the words of any of the old ballads I could remember the names of.

We have to do something, I roared in the middle of the road. I want to get out of my head, Danny.

We were both soaked by the rain. A car slowed down on seeing us and reversed.

We have to do something tonight. Let it all go.

He was leaning over the railings, shouting down to the river: Who are you kidding? Who the fuck are you kidding? The sea's the other way. You took a wrong turn.

He jerked his face towards me: Back-stabbers. Laughing behind their hands. Sniggerers. Back-stabbers.

Who?

The whole lot of them. This whole fucken city. All their talk's a . . . I don't want anything, you know that? Nothing. Just me and the rest of them can get lost.

Too right, I told him.

She saw right through me. And I know when it happened, he said and winked at me, one slow hideous closing of his eye that I thought he would never snap out of.

Danny?

When I touched her . . . that's when, he hissed through his teeth.

He held out his hands.

When I touched her. She could feel it in my hands.

We both stared at his trembling, outstretched hands, the rain hitting his palms, the delicate nails, and the nodding red light behind his fingers.

He dropped his arms slowly. His face was swollen and ugly and wet. He spoke to me with his eyes closed.

Remember that last night? That last night in London? Fucken London . . .

I pleaded with him to put it out of his mind.

Remember the state of me? What'd I do? I think I'd gone off my head, I mean it. I ran out of your place. All I did was . . . kept running . . . for ages. All over London like a mad dog. Streets and streets and streets. I hadn't a clue where I was. I scared myself shitless.

He paused and then opened one eye that was wild with a nameless imprecation: You know when something affects you?

I shrugged.

That it's only a matter of time. The way those streets in London were so strange and empty. You don't matter a fuck in it. That it's only a matter of time before everything feels like that . . . everything. Right down to your own streets, your own house, your own bed, people's faces. Yourself. Just as empty and foreign. And all the rest is just talk.

Naw, Danny, listen, I grabbed hold of him, almost sobbing into his face about the girl I had seen on the train coming back through France.

You should have seen her, Danny. This bliss in her eyes, luscious and pained. Like she wanted to explode with her own desire. About sixteen. She followed me out of the carriage. Her parents were sleeping in the carriage. She couldn't help it. It was pitch dark but I knew she was near me. Then this station we went through and a blaze of lights. She'd opened her shirt. No bra. The look on her face, Danny, like she was in pain with it. Like she couldn't take any more. Her eyes closed. There were her breasts and body in front of me. She had to have somebody see her, her mad pining turbulence. She was about to faint. Bursting point. And her hands were opening her jeans . . . and then it's pitch black again, Danny, and I can't move. I just have to stand there and I know she's still there, touching herself, moaning. Why Danny? I roared at him, shaking him by the coat. Why, for fuck's sake? Is it just a bad joke or what? It's everything and it can't last. Do you hear me?

4

I slept in the spare room of my brother's house with a view through the window of a side street and a dilapidated playground, the charred carcass of a roundabout and the chains wrapped to snapping point around the high bar of the swings. After the night out with Danny, I woke up aching and feverish. I lay in bed for three days. I think I got up once on the dusk of the first day and stood by the window as the street lights came on; they were candles at a sordid nativity. I was sickened with dread at the sense of my own loneliness. Figures passed along the street, hunched and ashamed of having to do anything, and the cars mortified them with lights. Downstairs, I heard my brother singing to his daughter.

He came into the room late one night when he thought I was asleep. For a long time he leaned against the door – so long that I eventually sat up and confronted him.

You hate sickness, don't you? You can't bear the presence of weakness.

I waited for his reaction.

Look at me, I said. A wreck. Pathetic. It revolts you, doesn't it?

There still was no response from him.

I remember one time I was sick when I was young and I woke you up, begging for some water. I had to beg you and beg you. You came back with a glass and told me to open my mouth. What was it you gave me? Do you remember, Michael? Vinegar.

And I'd do the same again, he said. This time and every time. So I'm not guilty. That's one of your philosophers, isn't it?

Are we going to have an intellectual debate? I jeered at him.

What are you doing back here? I want an answer.

After a long pause, I said: A dead end . . . I reached a dead end. In myself. I was living with this girl –

Spare me the details.

Suddenly I wanted to be able to tell him everything. I knelt up in the bed.

Listen to me, Michael. Let me tell you. Just listen to me. Please.

This is no place for you.

What? I said, dumbfounded.

Not for the likes of you. No hope.

I collapsed on the bed, hearing his breathing and the coins falling together in his pocket when he shifted his stance.

Mark my words, he said before he left, closing the door behind him. I heard him laughing with Martina in the hall a little while later.

I tried to dream of Valeria. Her face was usually fixed in front of me when I closed my eyes. Even my constant betrayals of her, with her best friend in the end, had not been enough to make her lose faith in me. She would do anything in her power to stop me debasing myself more than her. She refused to believe that she could have fallen in love with a coward and a liar; I was playing a joke on her, testing her faith. *Perché godi quando io ti giudico un codardo?* she moaned over and over again until she fell asleep. Under a white moon I sat on her balcony, peaceful and condemned, and made the ludicrous decision that I had lost the ability to feel guilty. From that moment on, I knew I would never catch up on my self again. Part of me was already prowling insanely through the cobbled streets.

PART TWO

We had been in pubs all day. Danny was celebrating getting the job in the hotel. By the time it was dark, we had both fallen into a slump of silence and bitterness. We went into the White Hat where we saw Lorna and some of her socialist friends (she used the word 'comrade' insistently). They had been to a lecture on James Connolly, I found out later. Danny pushed me in amongst them. The speaker I had seen at the demonstration was there, tapping his palm as he explained some principle to Lorna, who did not raise her eyes towards me.

Without hiding his drunkenness, Danny began to ask them ludicrous questions about the collapse of the ceasefire; it was obvious to me that he was letting on to know even less than he usually did. Danny would have looked at me with genuine incomprehension if I had tried to force him to confess to this.

Why don't the IRA just keep on with the ceasefire and show everybody that it's the Brits and the Loyalists that are stopping any progress? he put to the speaker. The moral high ground the papers call it, don't they? You know what my Ma says? The IRA are just afraid of getting what they want. They don't want to win because they'll have to turn into their own worst enemy. That's the kind of stupid thinking that gets this country nowhere, isn't it?

I went outside to get some air; I was tense and overexcited as if I were anticipating some fundamental loss of control. Earlier, Danny and I had been trying to remember the nights of drinking up back lanes and in derelict houses before we looked old enough to get into pubs – Danny recalled those nights with a grim forthrightness that left me feeling dispirited. The evening sky threatened to slide back into dusk. To my surprise, Lorna appeared in front of me on the street.

Folding her arms, she stepped closer and accused me of being drunk. Then came a stream of personal questions which I found myself comically trying to answer with some degree of honesty.

Is all that the truth?

I didn't understand why I wanted her to believe me. My attempts at speaking truthfully only added to my unease. She put her hands deep in the pockets of her long black coat and threw back her head, clotting the street air with the scent from the woven spire of her hair; she was wearing too much make-up and what I guessed were her favourite clothes: a loose black dress and a black silk shirt chosen to conceal her difficult bulk. She wasn't attractive to me but I was already entertaining the idea that I might be able to escape my heavy-handed narcissism in her company.

I'll believe it if you do, I told her, appearing unconcerned.

I don't trust you at all, she smiled. She had perfect lips, I noticed for the first time.

You're wearing a lot of make-up tonight. What are you all dressed up for?

Don't start that again, Lorna showed me her horseshoe frown. I wouldn't be talking to you at all if Danny hadn't asked me.

He's always trying to set me up. Everywhere we go he sends some woman over to talk to me. So what did he say to you? That I was just back and finding it hard and needing somebody to talk to.

She gave me a mock grin. You're very slick, she said.

You are, I went on in the same vein. You're the one taking advantage; here I am disorientated and vulnerable and then you accost me with a list of intimate questions. And what do I know about you? That you're obviously all dressed up, that you're a socialist and –

There's absolutely nothing else to know, she interrupted me vehemently.

She waited until I had stopped laughing. The street filled briefly with a crowd of teenage revellers. Some of them were dancing; one bleached blonde came near us and stared at Lorna with rapt curiosity. I was irritated by Lorna's embarrassment under this gaze. With the slightest incentive, we could have stepped into their midst and forgotten ourselves.

Some people have learned to enjoy themselves anyway, I said sarcastically as the young girl backed away from us – she was retreating, and pointing a warning finger, or a pledge, at us.

Lorna threw a disdainful look over her shoulder: Do you think so? They'll all be lying in the gutter in a few hours' time or battering each other over the head. Is that what you call enjoyment, then?

Before I could speak, she said in an almost absent-minded way: Something must have happened to bring you back.

She was studying me closely. I caught on instantly that she was testing the depths of my frivolity.

Something must have happened to keep you here, I replied.

I'll listen if you want somebody to talk to, she said solemnly, without moving her eyes from my face. Everyone deserves to be listened to. Once anyway.

What do you want to know?

Nothing. Just the normal things.

I'm tired of being listened to. I want to convince somebody – tear their heart open, I heard myself saying, revolted by the compassion in her eyes.

She nodded slowly in agreement but her mind seemed to be on something else. That's a big responsibility, she murmured almost to herself.

I burst out laughing again but she stood her ground before my mockery, gently examining me as though I was a banal hallucination or trick of the light that lacked the power to unsettle her. All around us, the night was being force-fed on drunken glee.

Maybe I came back to meet you, I grinned.

Her face shut itself up instantly behind a mask of outrage

27

and suspicion – the rapidity of this change impressed me so much that I let her go back inside without saying another word to her.

Much later, at a new club called The Ghetto, Danny and I danced with two girls who invited us back to their flat. One of them with oversized breasts let me kiss her against a wall where you could write your own graffiti. Her friend, who was much prettier, watched us with repugnance.

Just as we were about to leave, Danny took me aside. He didn't want to go, he said, shrugging repeatedly. At first I thought it was a problem with the girl but he claimed he just wasn't in the mood. His lethargic excuses infuriated me and I lost my temper with him; I was out of my mind on drink. He shrugged again and stumbled away towards a group of people around a table in the corner . . . I went after him to shout some more. Seeing Lorna in that corner only added to my frustration. The two girls had already left by this stage. I didn't know what to do to control myself. After a couple more drinks I wasn't feeling any calmer. I climbed up the metal stairs to one of the scaffold galleries and fell in with a crowd who were more determined to get off their heads.

Lorna said I came charging towards her, ordered some man to move to another chair and spent the next hour shouting incoherently into her ear. I don't remember any of this. When she couldn't get a taxi, she said, I began to follow her home, through the crowds, shouting at everybody. I was lucky not to get my head kicked in.

I have a memory of us both falling over on the street. Lorna was so devastated by shame at finding herself face down on the pavement that I followed behind her the rest of the way in silence.

2

I was living in a house in Belfast, a wee house with the stairs as narrow as . . . I was a student up there, Lorna said, shaking her head at the absurdity of the idea. I wanted to be a painter. Belfast? Laugh if you want. But it's just all rules and aesthetics. You weren't allowed to talk about emotion or reality or . . . This old man who lived next door used to come in to our kitchen when he was scared . . . and I'd sketch him. In secret. Isn't that terrible? Isn't that a terrible thing to do?

She was sitting on her doorstep. Nothing of what she was saying made much sense at the time. I listened only when it suited me. She was racked by a desire to explain herself to me, in an attempt to control me. I was still drunk and fervent after the club. With more aggression than I had yet seen in her, she let her hair down.

How are you supposed to do anything if there's no reality? she cried out suddenly, near to tears. Who's the winner there? And shooting every night of the week? That postmodernist game is just a way for people to ease their conscience.

What are you talking about? I shouted back at her. Do you think I care? Burn everything, that's the only answer.

You see, there's a socialism of the mind and a socialism of the heart, she went on in a different voice, calm and sententious. You only have to look around at –

What about the body? I bet you he wants to know about the socialism of your flesh, I said, walking up and down now in the small, dark street.

She closed her eyes until the dizziness had gone: What did you say? What?

He's after you. He's all over you. The sight of him depresses me.

Who? she moaned.

The speaker – Martin or Emmet or whoever. You were in the pub pretending to be engrossed by what he was saying.

What you're thinking is . . . ugly and – I wouldn't be worth him. I wouldn't be worth him. You neither. Not everybody's like us, you know. There's better people than us. Far better.

To my own surprise, I was shaken to my core by these words. I ran towards her like I would have done that day when she sank to her knees on the busy street, and the breath seized up in her as though she was trying to inhale the random glut of bullets from the building opposite, and she lay down in a shop door then, soundlessly, as gracefully as she could, wrapping her coat around her, and she left no trace, they said.

I grabbed her by the shoulders: Don't say that . . . If you say that . . .

All your talk in the club . . . she sneered at me. Just because you can say something, doesn't mean you can make it disappear. This city's not obsolete. Like chloroform, you said. Soporific. How dare you? Doldrums and diehards. Diehards. Who made it that way? Did you ever ask yourself why we're like this? Or are you too afraid to find it in yourself? You're from the dust bowl as well, keep that in mind. You're somebody else's nightmare if we all are. Judge yourself first.

It's impossible to judge yourself, I said glibly.

That's your excuse for hedonism is it?

She tried to push me away from her.

You don't know anything about my shame. You can't judge me, she said then.

What shame, Lorna? Why are you crying? I asked her, suddenly concerned at the tears pouring down her face. What have you got to be ashamed of?

You talk about dreams but you don't know anything about them, she shouted back. You've no idea. Because mine's all come true.

A disgusting grin changed the shape of her wet, ruined face.

You've no idea, she said in a sing-song voice this time.

Down on my knees in front of her, I got it into my head that it was necessary for her to hear the dream that had been torturing me since coming back to those withered streets – those streets that reminded me of nothing but the emptiness in myself.

. . . in a forest, Lorna, listen. I see a horde of children running around through the trees. It's night. They're all naked. I can hear their feet on the forest floor. Loads of pounding feet.

30

The pine needles are stuck to the soles of their feet and all over them like hair. A big bonfire they are dancing round – there's about fifty of them in the firelight . . .

I don't want to hear, she moaned, trying to get to her feet. This is where I live.

Lorna, listen. They're all dancing and I'm hiding, watching them. It's a feast, a celebration. But I'm spotted and they start chasing me . . . a gang of naked children. And I'm laughing because I think there's no danger. But then they catch me. They attack me, Lorna . . . and maul me and start ripping me to pieces with their hands and their mouths and teeth. I wake up frantic, looking for lumps taken out of me . . .

She was struggling to fit her key in the door.

What are you doing? I roared at her.

I have to go. I'm sorry.

You can't leave me alone now.

A look of abject misery appeared on her face; she was asking me to let her escape.

Your face, I said to her. You should see yourself. The disappointment.

Please. It's not with you.

I won't make it, I can't make it home. I'm scared . . .

She got herself inside the house before I could react. Enraged, I pounded on the door with my fists. My head was beating violently in time with my heart. Picking up a milk bottle, I smashed it on the step with some idea of throwing the glass through the letterbox. For a few moments I was empty and lulled, almost serene. I rolled up my sleeve and forced the broken neck into my skin until the blood trickled out along my arm. The idea of writing on her door did not enter my mind until I saw the blood dripping off my fingers.

With a bloody fingertip I wrote on the door: IMPATIENCE.

The sky was a repudiating spew of stars as I ranted and cursed between the rows of darkened houses that appeared to me like walls or barricades – the streets were moats of despair and silent striving. A green lovebite of a moon hung above the cathedral. Running in whatever direction took me, I began to harbour the idea of visiting my mother. It seemed so right after a while: I just had the wrong time that last day, that's all the trouble was, I chanted delightedly to myself. I would pull up a chair next to her, take her hand in mine and tell her everything. She would gaze compassionately at her son as he confessed to the pretentious disorder of his life. That the late hour might be any kind of obstacle didn't occur to me. I saw myself ringing a bell, a light coming on and the puffy, sallow face of a young nurse leaning out of the shadows. Taking my hand, she leads me through the naive dark of the corridors to my mother's door, where she leaves me with a modest, lopsided smile.

As I ran on through the dream-dry streets and came to the bottom of the hill, I still did not know what I wanted to confess. I'll make her laugh, see her laughing again, I was shouting, as though it was a shout of defiance to the buildings and the road and the parked cars and the wasted luxury of the night sky. I'll tell her stories of where I've been, the rococo cities and cave-filled mountains, men who have never prayed and women with eyes like sun on silk who longed for me to leave them, and she will lie back on her pillow and sigh and close her eyes and ask me to tell her once again.

The front entrance was in darkness: no one responded to the buzzer. I began to walk around the building, pressing my face against the windows like a madman. Through one window I saw a room in which there was a perfect circle of enormous orthopaedic chairs; I looked into an empty bed where the white pillows reminded me of eggs about to hatch; in the dining room the chairs stood on the tables like insects plotting an upheaval.

A light went on behind the curtained window I decided to knock on. Hello, I tried to call unthreateningly. Hello . . . but I knew my voice sounded hysterical and even comical. I'm just looking for somebody, Mrs O'Kelly. Do you know her . . . Mrs O'Kelly? I'm her . . . The light in the room went out. I fought to restrain myself from breaking the glass. Where are the nurses? I began to wonder; I'm making so much noise and nobody is checking to see. Then I walked around the outside of the building and banged indiscriminately on the windows, shouting: Where are the nurses? You have them all drugged. I'm going to report you. All lying in bed naked and drinking and fucking each other. Spotty bitches and washed-out gunmen. That's my mother you've got, greasy bitches. You're no better than screws . . . I'm just looking for somebody . . .

I heard nothing before a blanket of light was thrown over me. A voice shouted some words I couldn't understand – but the voice seemed to enter my body and inject panic into my heart. Running petrified across gravel, then grass, I could think only of the necessity of escape. I had never imagined such a degree of fear. On the wet grass, I skidded and fell backwards, got up again and ran on. People were shouting, but I thought they were encouraging me to run faster, to keep going because whatever was pursuing me was certainly not human. Behind me was a barrage of shifting hungry light.

Reaching a wall, I jumped and found a grip for my hands, a ledge for my feet (unusually for this city, there was no barbed wire or splintered glass along the top). The darkness of the laneway on the other side made me hesitate for some reason. Then, above me, I noticed the soft white fuel of the stars – I was sitting dumbfounded by something in the stars, one leg on either side of the wall. Another voice exploded near me but before I could tip myself over the edge, I was trapped by skewers of light coming from all sides.

They pulled me down from the wall. It was the RUC: one of the nurses in the home must have called to report a lunatic in the grounds. I was relieved to get out of the torchlight when they forced me against a wall, my lips touching the mossy stone, a pair of hands searching me, radios crackling. Nothing on him, a woman announced and then she handcuffed me, telling me how lucky I was, that I could have been shot.

The panic was gone, leaving me strangely tranquil and

brimming with a rare fulfilment. As she put the metal clamps on my wrists, I stared at the gentle ebullience of the stars, and marvelled at the happiness in my heart – I told myself that I had never felt happier, that I had been waiting on this. The stars swooped down on me with kisses in an orgy of sweetness and brought tears to my eyes. I was covered in muck from the grass. The cop pushed me along the dark lane. With my eyes on the heavens, before long I succeeded in falling headfirst to the ground. She knelt down and whispered unintelligible words into my ear that I took to be threats.

PART THREE

About a week later I was living in a bedsit in the centre of town, on the top floor of a narrow Victorian house with too many windows. A group of Spanish students occupied the rooms on the floor below me. The buildings on either side were concealed behind scaffolding and ropes and sheets of white plastic that buckled and slapped like gunfire in the relentless wind. During the months I lived there, I never saw a sign of anyone at work on these vivisected houses; it was the same all over the city, gutted shops and sliced-up streets left to wait under swathes of plastic and wire netting, like the traces of some disease were being kept out of view.

One morning, early morning when it was still dark, I was woken by the noise of fists hammering on my door . . . and there was Lorna, in her long black coat.

I stood shivering by the side of the bed, waiting for her to say her piece and then leave me alone. The room was freezing; in a fit of nervousness I began to suspect that I had already spent several months in the company of this woman, but that I could remember nothing since the night I had written on her door in blood. She lowered herself into the chair by the window, a queen on her shabby throne of pain, and merged at once with the darkness. It's too late to apologize, it all slipped my mind, I had the urge to shout at her. Instead I asked if she wanted a light turned on; my voice trembled with unintended mockery. It was about six in the morning. Outside the streets would be gnawing and sucking on their own emptiness.

I'm going back to bed, I said defiantly when she didn't answer. I felt trapped in my own room, waiting in the gloom for her dreadful verdict. I lay under the blankets, trying to control my agitation, but it was useless and I got up again and went out to the toilet in the hall for as long as I could, only to find that she hadn't moved from her black corner.

I practically shouted her name: Lorna.

I rushed towards her. Lifting her face to me – a violent glance stopped me in my tracks. I saw then that she was completely white.

Confused, I shouted at her again: What the hell is going on? Look at the state of you.

In the shadows, she lowered her head and mumbled.

What, Lorna?

I was scared, she screamed back at me. OK?

I looked at her angrily; I didn't know what to do.

Scared? I said meaninglessly. When I opened the curtains, the street light smouldered in the slimy branches of a dripping tree.

Lorna, you might think you're scared, but I don't even remember you ever being in this flat before. That's the kind of state my head is in. OK? I said vindictively as I got back into bed.

I haven't; Danny told me, she said softly, untroubled by the madness of what I was saying. What happened to your face?

Never mind my face. Danny told you what? To come and see me and talk it all out and tell me how you feel and make me pay and everything'll be great? Are you just going to sit there? Do you think you can make me suffer by staying silent? I don't remember. So whatever I did on you –

Danny told me where you lived – your address.

I don't remember seeing you since that night at your door, I went on. Do you hear me? So whatever I've done since on you, I'm not going to apologize for. You wake me up and then sit there all wounded as though you're entitled to something. Come on, tell me what I did on you so I can go back to sleep. What do you want me to say sorry for?

Lorna stayed quiet, wrapped in her coat.

Then she said: I'm sorry. I shouldn't have come.

What should you have done then? I asked sarcastically. Am I not repentant enough?

I don't know what you're talking about, Niall. I haven't seen you since that night either. I just needed – I just panicked that's all . . . that's all, she said with profound weariness.

A light came on in a house across the street; I found myself enviously imagining a man who, as he opens his eyes, discovers that he is deliciously aroused by the thought that there will be many other mornings exactly the same, and gropes in the warmth for the breast of his sleeping wife. I lay down on my back and stared at the discoloured ceiling. The thought of the life I had left to live petrified me.

I'm sorry, I heard Lorna say. There was just . . .

I've nothing to say to you, I told her, purely to increase the atmosphere of gloom.

A few intolerable seconds later she said: Who could blame you?

Cruelly, I remained silent, deciding to let her stew in her own guilt – she suffered intense guilt whenever she wanted to talk about herself. The rationality with which she crushed the world around her was completely useless against herself. I knew that on occasions like these she felt ugly, corrupted, almost evil.

I heard that your brother threw you out of the house, she said tentatively some time later. Was it bad?

I laughed, refusing to allow her the penance of listening to me – she encouraged me to babble on so much because it alleviated her own guilt for wanting to talk about her own miseries.

Is it just you and him? I know his wife Martina. Just to see, like. They have a wee girl, don't they? Were you ever close to him . . . when you were younger?

When I didn't answer, she went on: I've a brother in Australia. Three children. Every year we get another set of photos. I mind the last time he was back; he came down the stairs and looked out the window at the rain and he says, Why the hell does anybody bother living here? It sums him up perfectly.

I searched the lustreless dark for her face, wondering what she was struggling to tell me. All I could make out was the deeper shade of her hair and her formless body, which brought to mind the word *denier*. The dark was about 90 denier now and Lorna was about 500 denier.

Lorna, if you have something to say then get on with it, I demanded.

I don't know if I've anything to say either, she replied, laughing at herself. I don't know what I'm doing here. Something came into my head when I was coming round here that I haven't thought about in ages.

For a few minutes she didn't say a word. I had almost fallen back asleep when I heard her voice again, sharp and jabbing and sporadic: I was standing outside our house one day on the Lecky Road. I was only about six. I had my face up into the sun with my eyes shut, feeling the warmth and . . . Then I felt this hand touching me. On my shoulder. Then this voice, a man's voice. Just you stand still there, love, he says. Don't move, all right; just keep your eyes closed there. I thought it was the sun talking to me. I felt this hard thing on my shoulder. He was kneeling down behind me and he keeps whispering to me not to move and everything's all right. The sun's getting hotter and hotter on my eyes and making me dizzy. That's all I could feel . . . and then his breath on the back of my neck. He'd been eating bacon. He was touching my hip and I thought I was going to faint. Then I just couldn't bear it any more and opened my eyes. Across the street there was this woman – why am I telling you this anyway? she interrupted herself, laughing again. I only thought about it on the way round here. It's not something I think about a lot or anything. You could have been here with somebody.

When I woke up, Lorna was standing at the bottom of the bed. It troubled me to think how long she might have been watching me, the frayed ropes of hair dangling across her face, which was pale and bloated. A vibrant blue sky filled the window for a second and then was covered over by cloud. The gulls were screaming above the street. I pretended to be still lost in a dream.

So tell me what happened to your face.

I still bore the marks of falling over again and again, hand-cuffed and rejoicing, as the cops tried to get me into a Land-Rover.

Female? Those scratches look female, she said, as she made a scrupulous survey of my face.

Hiding behind my hands, I grumbled some words in Italian.

I'll mind my own business, then.

To wind her up, I said: This fella was saying he thought we were all doomed to extinction unless there's a minimum wage. It was purely political.

The poignancy of her gaze seemed to shunt me forcefully backwards out of the world to some place where my suffering was not entirely my own.

You going to work? I said to distract her.

She blinked herself back into the bedroom, and nodded. I have to go back and get my stuff, she said. I'm giving them a slide show today. Duchamp and the Dadaists. The famous toilet.

I can't see you as a teacher. I just can't see it.

She nodded miserably. I wanted to shout at her.

I'm sorry about telling you all that. About that man when I was a girl. She formed her horseshoe frown.

Did you know who he was? I asked, struggling to remember her story. The fresh cloud poured past the window, letting through blinding patches of blue. It was impossible to tell if she was aware that I had fallen asleep before she had reached the point of it.

But touching you up in broad daylight? You must have got a look at him or . . .

She looked at me strangely, almost as though I was a child, and she smiled sadly then.

So who was he then?

It doesn't matter. I didn't really get a look at him anyway.

She tried to make it sound inconsequential. But in her eyes – catching sight of the moist, lonely tremor in her eyes, I wanted to touch her.

I started to talk: There was this day with our Michael and me and my Da when we were driving over the border. I think it must have been my first time in the Republic because I was sure I could see all these signs of freedom and joy in the trees and the shape of the hills and the colour of the sky. Everything seemed brighter. Anyway, we had our dog, Savannah, locked in the boot. It was completely off its head. Deranged. Michael and me are all excited anyway and my Da pulls up at the side of the road, tells us to stay put and disappears for a few minutes. The engine was still running and our Michael dared me to have a go at driving. He was always daring me to do things he didn't have the courage to do himself. He was the good one. But he was my big brother so I had no choice but to get into the driving seat. I don't know what I did but the car started moving. We were rolling back into the road. My Da starts running after the car and Savannah, who's out of the boot now, starts jumping on my Da and getting in the way. We were watching all this out the back window. And then my Da stops, tries to give the dog a kick, misses, falls over, gets back up again and throws up his hands in despair. Then off he goes walking away in the other direction and just leaves us in the moving car.

Laughing hoarsely, Lorna was covering her mouth with her hand: He just walked away? I don't believe you. What happened?

We went right across the road and crashed into a tree.

I don't believe a word, she insisted, giving me a long smile that was both sceptical and tender. So is this your funny side?

All of a sudden I was acutely embarrassed, sprawled in my bed while she stood over me, giggling then coughing, with the sky pouring by behind her. I didn't like her laugh: I always felt embarrassed when I made her laugh. Her confusion had no effect on me when I reminded her that she had failed to explain what she was doing in my flat.

The story was not entirely true either. The real story was that my Da drove Michael and me across the border to teach us a lesson. He took Savannah out of the boot, threw a stick into a river and when Savannah jumped in after it, my Da ordered us back into the car and drove off. That's what you get when you ruin a dog's temper, he said, wiping the sweat from his forehead with one of his handkerchiefs he always ironed himself. He was a short bald man with glasses, always doing everything at a pace that was too slow to watch for long without feeling exasperated by him.

I'm sorry . . . For just turning up, Lorna added. You must think I'm off my head.

That's what you want me to think, I told her, although I didn't believe this.

She searched in her coat pockets and then started to put in her earrings.

I'm going to sleep all day.

I wish I could, she said with a shocking surge of yearning that made me worry she would take the day off college and ask to spend it with me. I couldn't shake the feeling of exhaustion. Turning over in the bed, I pretended to go straight to sleep; I was listening to her moving about, fixing herself up again to be seen on the street, the annoying racket of her jewellery.

Before she went, she asked me what I was doing later. Sleeping, I said. It's the only thing that doesn't get me into trouble.

Don't bet on it, she warned me in such a way that I sat up in the bed, shocked by her chastening, raised eyebrow.

If you get bored, you know where I am, she said then, but spoiled this new flirtatious tone by adding: You have to let me make it up to you for this morning.

I asked her: Will boredom still exist after the revolution?

She must have thought I was mocking her, and left with a sad, self-effacing look back at me. I can't remember the colour of her eyes.

43

I met Martina by chance on the street and persuaded her to come with me to a café. We chose a place within the city walls, a secluded cobbled square built for the tourists. We took a table in a corner, hidden behind a display of bleached crab pots: I made a joke that we were behaving like illicit lovers.

She seemed tired and preoccupied, but she insisted there was nothing wrong. A white seam of scalp ran down the centre of her head I wanted to trace my finger along. We ordered some tea; she nodded lethargically as I tried to explain what had happened the night the cops brought me home, the drunken desire to see my mother.

There was nothing I could do, Martina said, meaning the way she had sat at the bottom of the stairs with her head in her hands while Michael was ordering me to have cleared out of the house before he got back from work the next day.

She suddenly showed her annoyance: What did you expect anyway, Niall? You brought the police round to the house for God's sake? That's what sent him mad. Then –

I didn't actually invite them, I said, trying to make light of it. They would have locked me up.

I saw Martina control her tongue in time and then withdraw her eyes – her long-lashed eyes shining with the strain of preventing herself from cursing the police, me, and what she was doing even talking to me.

This tea's cold, she said and dropped her spoon noisily on the table. A wizened woman in a pink fluffy scarf looked over at us; Martina ignored the woman's obvious hankering to speak to her.

Who doesn't? Martina told me when I asked her if they knew each other. Sure she used to be a teacher up in Creggan. She's a wino – and a few other things. Her husband moved out to Strabane with the wains. Don't look at her, she snapped at me.

Is that what's bothering you? Her?

Niall, what possible difference does it make to you what's bothering me? What do you want to know for? Really? She seemed frightened by her own tone of voice.

I'm sorry, I said.

She leaned towards me: So am I. I'm a woman with a husband and a child . . . a depressed husband and a child who won't eat and I'm guaranteed to spend the rest of my life in this place. Does that make you feel better now?

I'm sorry, I said again. You shouldn't even be sitting here. Michael would –

Niall, catch yourself on, will you? Just quit all the drama. You're not doing yourself any favours. I'm glad to see you back but you can't run around behaving like there's no consequences to your actions. Maybe in Italy or wherever, but not here. It's lucky your poor mother won't find out

The old teacher had come over to our table without us noticing. With a bizarre look on her face as though she thought she was surprising us, she asked if we had any spare change; her mouth was caked with the stains of different lipsticks. Martina wouldn't even meet her eyes as she slid fifty pence across the table. The old woman put her hand on my shoulder; I found a degree of comfort in the sight of the dirt in the wrinkles on her fingers and under her nails.

To think that woman taught most of the mothers in this city to read and write. Martina's face stiffened with hatred as she watched the old drunken prostitute gyrating slowly to a song on the radio at the counter. I could not remember Martina ever allowing an emotion of that kind to take hold of her.

I'll talk to him if you want me to, Martina, I said.

She searched in her pockets for some tissue and blew her nose. So how long do you think you're going to stay?

I shrugged.

She pretended to find this amusing; she shook her head and pursed her lips like an old woman. Maybe I'm worse than the two of you put together.

45

Don't say that, I told her.

She made a face of disillusion at herself. Maybe I am. Wanting everything to be all right and everybody to get on. It probably starts more fights than anything else. Treating everyone like they're wains.

I didn't come back to have it out with him, Martina. I don't know what there is to say, even. He's raging at me. What can I do?

Just stay away from him for a while. She sighed, wrapped her coat around her and suddenly began to tell me about an incident in a shop that morning when she had been trying to change a dress she had bought for Louise.

I felt powerless to help her; the very sight of me troubled her, grieved her, but she remained on her guard against me. I think she saw me as a wounded animal that she didn't have the heart to put out of its misery. You should never have come back here, I told myself as she lost herself in the details of the shopping story. Afterwards, I set myself the task of taking a casual *giro* around the city centre, to stroll about among the shoppers, the pensioners, and the unemployed, but my inveterate edginess and paranoia got the better of me and soon enough I was making my way quickly back to my flat.

I slept for most of the afternoon because it was dusk when I sat up in bed, startled, panting, with no memory of why. I had not bothered to undress. Suddenly the prospect of being alone in that room for the rest of the night was too much for me; the bed, the chair by the dirty window, the damp carpet, the doorless arch into the kitchen where the shadows were gathering and twisting slowly and hinting at words – everything seemed to be more real than I was. I was sure I was going to lose my mind. A minute later, I was back out in the street, in a light mizzle, with the black yoke of the dusk breaking across the sky.

Without trying to stop myself, I was heading out of the city, towards the fields and the back roads into the hills; the low bare hills formed a rotten defunct horizon around the city. Peacefully, the rush-hour crowds filled the streets to satiety.

The dusk oozed out above us all. We caught each other's eyes and lowered our heads in disgrace, and our stomachs turned over with the fear that suffering would never unite us. Hurrying amongst them, I saw myself sprawled in the heather on the side of a hill, a sky overburdened with stars, no moon, and the wind dancing among the old stones – at the time I believed I would be able to think clearly if I made it out of the city.

I wished Danny was with me. It would have been good to hear him talk about the nights when we used to walk out to the pagan fort, not far over the border. Freezing, rain-choked nights when we had finished our carry-out of cider and resigned ourselves to the malicious fact that nothing was going to happen, that nothing was even conceivable: no girls, no music, no fights, nowhere to go but another corner of another street. Often without speaking at all, we walked the few miles through the country lanes in the cramped darkness. At the circular fort, we found a place out of the wind, and smoked the last of our cigarettes. Nothing ever happened up there, either. We rarely wanted to talk. The rain hammered the luminous drums of fungus among the stones and the gorse but the ghosts were never tempted out. Numb with the cold, each of us thought only about the length and exertion of the walk back into Derry. Perhaps it was only the despairing job of the walk back that took us up there.

There was a man walking in front of me on the street who caught my attention for some reason. The dusk was giving way to a younger darkness, svelte and crisp, charged with spring. We were nearing the outskirts out the city; there were only a few people left on the streets. The man walked at a slow pace, as if he could take another direction on a whim, swinging a battered leather satchel and smiling fondly at whatever met his eye. I could tell that he was happy, that during the day he had been given good news, or a letter, a promotion or a dreamed-of flirtatious glance and he had not been able to concentrate on his work. And now he was taking his time about getting home, enjoying the breeze and misty rain on his face and the way his own shadow was swiped from under him by the car headlights.

At the steps to a boarded-up building (it was an old church hall) he stopped and read through the graffiti. I stood by a bus stop, watching him, the excitement trembling in my guts. A woman on her way by looked straight at him but he was too absorbed to notice her. After a few minutes, the man moved towards the steps and began to climb with inordinate care up to the door . . . He reached the top step – I saw then that he was not interested in the haphazard and arcane declarations of love and rage sprayed across the front of the building.

On the top step there was an upright collection of old emptied tins of beer, five of them, two of them half-crushed by a fist, and a coat rolled up in a corner; these were what he was looking at. I wanted to applaud him; I thought he was hoping to steal a sly drink, raise an illicit toast to his new happiness. I've been waiting on this, I said to myself, hardly able to keep still. I'll join in with him once he's started; we'll go and find a bar, I'll be able to talk to him.

For longer than I could tolerate, he looked down at the cans at his feet. As I watched him, he tipped one of the cans over with his toe and followed it down the steps where he nudged it again. There must be nothing in it, I thought for he went back up again with the same carefulness to the top step. He knocked over a second can then, and again followed in its wake to the pavement, where he helped it on its way into the gutter. I was bewildered. He did the same with the third can. On the fourth, it dawned on me what he was doing – picking up the fourth, he poured a trickle of beer onto the ground . . . Then he went up to get the last, stepping over the puddle of beer. He was making sure the cans were empty. Yes, he was making sure there was nothing left; he was making sure that as he lay in bed that night he would hear the wailed-out agony of the old drunks denied the last flat dribble of drink to see them through to the light.

48

I ran up behind him and attacked him. He went down without a noise, like I was pulling clothes off a line, and I kicked him a few times and ran away. I was demented; I couldn't believe what I had seen, or what it meant, or the pain it was causing me. Gasping and laughing at the same time, I didn't know which idea was more unbelievable, that this was a random act of purity or was it a nightly habit? I had never imagined anything so meticulous, so pious, so lonely. My mind was crowded with images of what I should have done to him, the purifier, the boots and punches I should have inflicted on him, a paving stone clawed up and dropped on his head, tearing him to pieces and smearing his blood and filth across all the lintels of the city.

Eventually I found myself in an area of the city I didn't know, a housing estate. I was still wiping away my tears when I approached two teenage girls sitting on a wall. They wanted to know if I was all right: all I could do was point towards the way I had come. They thought I was indicating that I was being chased and began to look nervous. I shook my head but couldn't explain myself. The two of them had a fit of giggling and tried flirting with me, asking me for cigarettes. They didn't care about the distress I was in.

I'm not being funny, I stuttered, I'm not . . . I saw this man . . .

Was he good-looking? one of them laughed.

Do you know she's not wearing any knickers? the other said, and tried to pull up her friend's skirt. They were clawing at each other and having hysterics.

Without warning, both of them stopped and glared at me suspiciously, their faces flushed.

Do you want your eyes back? one of them said.

Give us a fag?

Have you got a wee dick? We don't like big ones. Do we?

Maybe he's one of them bum-merchants.

Where's your handbag, love?

Arm in arm they walked out into the street, and there they turned around and began to call names at me and threaten me with their brothers and their fathers; they said they were going to tell them straight away. One of them picked up a stone. She threw it at me.

3

Lorna and some of her comrade friends, about eight of them, were watching a band in the upstairs room of a pub in town. Their wry smirks made it clear that she had been talking about me. Without a doubt I looked in a terrible state, agitated and washed out. All I wanted was to forget myself in a crowd of people. Lorna scrutinized me: she was gratified to see the mess I was in, but I had no strength left to challenge her. A mute depression had taken over me after the euphoria of earlier; I must have walked around for hours in those housing estates, waiting to be lynched.

I stood in a crowd near the bar, incapable of pushing my way through to order a drink. The place had a low curved ceiling; I was leaning against anyone who didn't move away. On the small stage, the singer was hopping around and thumping a bodhrán with his hand. Lorna hooked her big arm in mine, pressing her breasts against me. I wanted to ask her to take me home; the words echoed loudly inside me but they wouldn't come out. That morning I had found an envelope pushed under my door, and inside a frail sheet of blue paper smelling of her bleary scent where she had written to tell me she was going out to hear some music that evening. I've forgotten all about the other morning so there's nothing to apologize for, she added at the bottom under her name; she signed her name in full, *Lorna McNulty*, in a rounded dramatic hand. The paper was so thin it had ripped as she made a final flourish on the tail of the *y*.

She bought some drinks and I followed her back to the table. The speaker nodded to me as though we knew each other. There was a pile of socialist newspapers on the chair next to him. He bothered me with his self-containment.

Lorna, on the other hand, grew extremely animated; she was sweating and laughing, orchestrating most of the conversation around the table. The others listened to her with a mixture of awe and malicious glee at her liveliness, which they sensed would disgrace her. In my dejected mood, I tried to find her beautiful, dressed all in black, her hair in two tightly wound ponytails. She refused to let me remain silent; I was drinking as quickly as I could. She kept telling everyone around the table about me (she was shouting above the music), that I had been away, that I hated being back, and I was a writer. The others mostly smiled or watched the band to hide their embarrassment.

Why are you laughing like that? I said to Lorna, irritated by the way it went on for too long.

Like what?

The speaker was tapping the rim of his glass against his teeth.

You don't mean it, I told her. No one else feels like laughing when you laugh. You're faking it.

As I said this, I knew it wasn't the right description. It dawned on me at that moment that I knew nothing about myself or her or anyone else in the upstairs bar; this thought turned me on and I imagined a violent orgy unfolding before me.

Show me your laugh then, Lorna said and started to tickle my ribs. I pushed her away but she wouldn't stop.

Tickle, tickle, tickle, she was saying in an annoying voice, nipping at me with her fingers.

I had to get up from the table to escape her and – I thought I was going to hit her. Back to the bar, I ordered some whiskey. I'll drink this and go, I told myself; this is a big mistake. I was sure she had asked me to come to take her revenge on me.

When the band was finished, Lorna found me again in the narrow corridor that led to the toilets. Here, the ceiling was decorated by a badly painted *trompe l'œil* of swans with the faces of children drifting across a gloomy lake. I had forgotten what I had been talking about.

Do you think I'm drunk? Am I flirting with you, do you think? Just because a girl knocks on your door at six in the morning doesn't mean anything, you know. Lorna gave me a travesty of a promiscuous stare and moved towards me.

She was near enough now for me to see the grains of powder on her big face, the scarlet scree of lipstick at the corner of her mouth, the overlarge nostrils, the white patches under her eyes, her uneven hairline.

Are you still being angry with me for tickling you?

I tried to convince myself that I found her attractive. I wanted some company other than my own. She was waiting on me to kiss her.

Tell me something. Anything. What did you do today? Were you writing?

I gave her a dry look.

No don't, she said like a girl. Don't be annoyed with me. I'm so clumsy. I'm . . .

She put her hands on my shoulders.

Tell me I'm not clumsy, she said, feigning an expression of innocence.

I saw this man tonight, I began to tell her, remembering what I had wanted to say earlier. Up the Culmore Road at the old church hall.

What were you doing way up there? she asked with exaggerated interest.

There were these old beer cans on the steps where this crowd of alcos must hang out. (As I was saying this, I knew that I had no chance of making her understand what I had seen.) This man anyway, he stops and empties all the cans out, the last dregs. He was just passing and he stops to make sure they're all completely empty . . . in case . . .

The story didn't seem important to me any more, either.

You get all types, said Lorna, for something to say. She was looking the other way.

Nothing makes the least bit of sense, I said ridiculously.

She moved nearer me again. What's the matter? You look like you've seen a ghost.

I let her kiss me; her mouth was sour, her tongue coated in a thick stale saliva. Then she pulled away and made a ghost noise into my ear; she fell into a fit of laughing. An earring was caught up in her hair.

Holding my hand, we went back to join the others at the table. The singer from the band was sitting there, talking about the bomb in London that had ended the ceasefire; he had been to see the devastated office building, he told us, and his girlfriend had filled her pockets with glass debris and made a glittering mobile for her bedroom. This idea caused exasperation around the table. The singer, who had a London-Irish accent, appeared to be at a loss that no one saw the funny side of this.

From there the talk moved on to whether the socialist group should be seen to join in with a Sinn Féin rally. Tapping his palm, the speaker began to elucidate the major points with his hairless white fingers; every time he corrected the position of his glasses, I thought of somebody trying to remember how to bless themselves properly. While he was talking, Lorna nodded enthusiastically and peered into every face around the table for affirmation. They were all desperate to find something interesting to say. Watching her, I felt the same suffocation as when she laughed; I longed to tell the table about the young woman who had had to hide from her dreams in my room until the morning light came and emptied her head.

I was listening to her rave about some painter when the speaker moved in beside me. Lorna and he talked across me for a while; I was still gulping down drink.

So you've been away travelling? He finally decided it was the right time to speak to me.

I gave a meaningless snort. It made me nervous to have them on either side of me.

I've never got around to it, he went on. One day, maybe. I'd need a good reason though, that's my problem. Some people can just go off and wander. I wish I was more like that and could just lie on a beach and –

No you don't, Emmet, Lorna cried with a peculiar alarmed moan. She was staring at both of us as though she was transfixed by some idea in her head.

The speaker coughed. I wanted to ask for your point of view on all this, he said to me confidentially. You've been sitting there listening. Another perspective on all this would be useful.

Lorna gave a squeal of delight which made the two of us jump. Too right, she said and slapped my knee. What do you think of it all, Niall?

I reached again for my pint: About what?

The Black North, he said, attempting to be sarcastic. Has the opportunity been lost for good?

I had nowhere to look other than at a young couple at the opposite table who were leaning towards each other, kissing, their elbows on their knees.

You see, the speaker went on . . . the IRA lost patience. Anybody can see the British messed it up. They're still held to ransom. Or maybe it's all the fault of the Irish government's lack of will. But what we have to do as socialists is look forward beyond all the doomsday scenarios, speculate, use our imagination. For example, let's say there was to be talks, new talks, and they all made some kind of agreement; well, it's easy to see that the minute they agree, and there's peace and democracy and the rest, then all those parties disintegrate. They would fall apart. It's that simple. They have no content. Because –

They're all sectarian, Lorna finished off for him.

There'd be room for a new kind of ideological politics here. This is one of the most politicized electorates in Europe. People would be open to radical alternatives. Socialism, communism, anarchism even. That's what the bosses are afraid of. I'm not saying anything new here really, am I? You'll have heard all this before.

With peace will come socialism, said Lorna. And why? Because there's absolutely nothing else on offer. And because it's right.

The two of them eyed me expectantly. I made myself smile; the boy must have tried to touch the girl's breast because she was now turning away from him with her arms folded and he was begging to be forgiven, touching her bare freckled shoulder, whispering to her, while scanning the room with a drunken proprietorial leer for his friends who he hoped would be watching.

Irritatingly, Lorna nudged me with her elbow, and said: Come on, Niall. Enough of the apolitical writer's stance. Or are you one of those who think that only a war will sort it all out?

I was trying to stay calm, sure they were intent on making a fool out of me.

Socialism is all about the long term, the speaker continued, touching his glasses excitedly for he had obviously just had some idea or other. What did James Joyce say: Silence, cunning and . . . Did you know he translated Oscar Wilde's defence of socialism into Italian? I only found that out the other day. We're going to do a piece on Wilde for the paper. He was a socialist, you know?

(He was saying all this with a note of triumph in his voice.)

He's not taking us seriously, Lorna sighed, and folded her arms. He's grinning to himself. What are you grinning at? The true meaning of all social phenomena is their position in the class struggle.

The girl on the stool was crying, her head against the boy's shoulder; he was awkwardly stroking her long bleached hair. I had no idea I was grinning – I felt a powerful compassion for the girl, her guilt and her volatile awareness of the desires that could destroy her . . . and the boy also, his thin strained face, his stealth and fear, his longing to be admired. As I watched, they began to kiss each other again.

Come on. You can't live outside these issues. What do you think? Lorna persisted, nudging me again.

Making it up on the spot, I said: I think the servant has taken her looking glass and she's sitting on it and watching it cloud over with the heat from her own fanny.

The table went silent. Lorna was the first to laugh but her face betrayed her confusion. I gloated on the idea that I had disappointed her. The speaker smiled and nodded as though he was in on the joke but his small blue eyes darkened with hostility.

And the master, I went on like a fool, is sitting on the other side of the room wanking himself off.

He's trying to wind us up, Lorna told the table. He's talking down to us. We're not worth a decent answer.

The speaker took off his glasses and blinked convulsively as he made up his mind what he should say, whether he should go in for the kill or talk to somebody else.

I suppose we lack imagination, Lorna said with ugly sarcasm.

I think I see what you mean, the speaker said with a theatrical sigh. Hegel you're talking about, isn't it? But we have to identify the master. That's the problem. As I said, we'll have to wait . . . the most difficult thing for us all is patience . . .

From out of nowhere, I was suddenly incensed by their air of sanctimonious defeat.

I started to rant at them: The cold-blooded murder of some stinking old woman or fucked-up teenager or . . . in the service of true freedom doesn't bother me one bit. Anyone who says it does is a hypocrite. You and your pathetic heroes – you can take your Prometheus and his fire and his culture and . . . I don't want anything to do with it. It makes me sick. You want slaves and work and work and work and moderation in all things. You don't know what greed is. You're afraid of anything you can't control. You'd shit yourself if there was a real revolution, an all-out strike on everything. There's other heroes, the mad impatient ones – saints of impatience, that's what I think and . . .

I kept on like this without any idea of what I was saying. All I knew was that they both infuriated me. Lorna with her big hair and spicy scent and mournful heart and him with his fraying jumper and his glasses and prodding crafty eyes. I

56

was shouting about greed or something like it; then I kicked over the table. All my compassion at the sight of the teenage lovers had vanished; now they looked scrawny and sneaky and doomed to bitterness.

It didn't take long for the bouncers to get their hands on me. Screaming with pure rage as they dragged me out of the door, I went on abusing the speaker as though he had insulted me to some unimaginable degree. The bouncers were almost impressed at the extent of my anger; they were genuinely curious to know what someone could have said to have got me into this state.

I was dumped outside. Lorna stepped out after a few minutes; I was sitting on the ground trying to get my breath back. Straight away, she started shouting at me: Who do you think you are? Who gives you the right to treat people like that? You have no right. Do you hear me? Can't you take being asked a question? You're the coward.

Her indignation made me calm down.

Did you tell them about the door? I wanted to know.

What door?

About me writing on the door? I screamed back at her. It wasn't clear to me if I'd been thinking about this all evening.

No.

Tell me the truth.

Niall, I haven't told them anything about us. I promise you. I met you at the demo, that's all they know.

You're lying . . . You're lying. You were all having a great laugh at me. Wheel him in and we'll see what he's made of.

Lorna shook her head speechlessly but I didn't believe her.

Don't con yourself, that's what you were doing.

She leaned her forehead against the wall. Please don't do this, I heard her saying, I'm sorry. Maybe you're right. Don't shout at me. I don't know what's happening.

Her acceptance of whatever I said only made me more vicious. Her weakness was gluttonous and deadly. All I could do was walk up and down shouting abuse at her, about her socialism, her loneliness and her pathetic dreams of tragedy.

I walked away eventually.

The streets were teeming with people, drunk and raucous. They gathered in groups, unwilling to go home, with all sorts of glasses in their hands – it could have been a chaotic night-time procession through the city, with glasses instead of candles or flowers, to a vigil in the main square. Bursts of song or fighting started at the slightest provocation. I was delirious, the effects of drink enhanced by my fit of anger. There were signs of disorder everywhere I looked: a rampant couple on the roof of a chip van, people gathering in doorways or on their knees, staring furiously at the ground; men pissed freely, writing their names on the walls; taxis revved their engines to get through the crowds. In spite of the numbers on the street, the bars were far from empty. Stooping among them, I fantasized about a widespread eruption of discontent, about the deity being called down from the skies and punished for stinginess in the streets. A cop Land-Rover kept at a safe distance in a car park. One bar seemed crowded with people in their forties; I had heard it said that the women in that place wrote their price for the night on the soles of their high heels. Suddenly a gang of young men in only their shirts surrounded me; before I could react they had moved on in search of some other victim. Some girl was screaming at everyone for no apparent reason. A fight broke out and then disintegrated with breathtaking delicacy like a moving swarm, or wind on water, or a gang of shoplifters in the new shopping centre . . . and broke out again in another part of the main road. I watched a teenager vomit into his girlfriend's hands . . . she then threw the handful of the stuff into the faces of people near her. I walked on and found the same in another street – dressed-up sweating crowds stunned at being cast back on the streets, panting, reckless, elated and distraught, going all out to fight off the sense of another failed attempt to overcome their limits, their dreams, and the city that always keeps its fingers crossed behind its back.

A girl stumbled against me; I caught her by the hands. She could barely manage to open her eyes. Her friend asked me to help them get a taxi. Neither of them had any charm or prettiness for me.

Where are you going to? the friend asked me.

Anywhere, I said for the laugh.

What are you doing on your own, anyway? Did you have a fight with her?

She won't let me touch her.

I'll touch you, the pissed one said and threw her arms around my neck. I'm so drunk you could do anything to me . . . I'm the dirtiest bitch in this . . . she slurred, without opening her eyes, laughing at herself.

Go ahead if you want, the friend sneered at me.

There was no chance of a cab, so we started walking. They were heading up to Rosemount where they had a flat. At one point we took a rest near the Fire Station, leaving the drunk one, who was telling stories of what an old boyfriend had made her do, lying on a wall where she was soon snoring.

I started kissing the friend and she went for my trousers without a second thought. Whether it was because I wasn't attracted by her or whether it was the drink, I couldn't get myself hard. At a loss about how to conceal her frustration, she pulled up her top and showed me her breasts – her breasts were small and too far apart.

Or is it her you want? she said, sneering at the one on the wall. She's making it all up, you know. She hasn't had a man in ten months. She's out of her head.

I don't know, I said. Do you want me to try?

You're a dirty bastard, she told me with slurred sincerity.

I risked it and said I was.

We'll go back to the flat and try, come on . . . come on, she grabbed at me with surprising strength.

In her bedroom she watched me undress her unconscious friend on the bed (I had asked her to masturbate while she watched but she refused outright). She had stripped down to her underwear, which looked bland to me. I couldn't get aroused with either of them, even when I tried to pull myself off over the both of them naked under me on the single bed. I had reached an unbearable level – my frustration was making me sick and filling my head with violent images. Outside in the street, I knelt between two parked cars and tried again to come, coaxing Valeria and her dark lush plumage back into my mind.

Still unsatisfied, I dragged myself through the deserted streets. Whatever I laid eyes on, the smooth brownish puss of sky, street lights, a woman's bra hanging in a tree, seemed to have the sole purpose of blocking my escape out of myself. Without noticing it, I had begun to think about London and the extraordinary loneliness of my first months there when I went to university. It was obvious to me now that it was loneliness that had made me drop out, although for years I had called it boredom or complained about the course. That period of my life in London was impossible to remember because I was entirely alone. Without taking any decision, I had ended up in a bedsit in Hackney, lying in bed all day, reading through the night, talking to nobody. It must have lasted for nearly a year. Then I met Caroline, in the library one day, my only outing other than signing on; she was looking for books on civil disobedience. She took me back to the squat where she lived with about ten others and a pack of stray dogs. In Spain, a few years later, I heard that she had fallen off a roof, out of her mind on mushrooms, and broken her skull.

I was unable to tell the story of my life – the pieces I tried to put together didn't convince me. Meeting Caroline, who shook the misery out of me, had as much significance for me as the bra dangling from the branches of the tree – it was simply another obstacle, another barricade. I had the feeling that my life was a slow process of suffocation. Just then, I turned a corner and saw a burning incandescent arch right in front of me. My heart immediately lit up and I ran towards the flaming portal with delight. A van was burning in the middle of the street, ferocious and final; that was all. Further on, a line of cop wagons waited out of sight in a side street.

4

Danny hid the book he was reading under the counter when I knocked on the glass door. He was wearing a brown suit. Keeping a hold on the door and eyeing the street like it could possibly be tricking him, he hurried me inside. It had been a week since I had seen him. In a comical whisper, he explained to me that there had been threats made against the hotel; most of the rooms were empty, he told me, casting his eyes upwards. I hadn't been drinking that day but I'd started smoking some grass at dusk and I felt giddy and innocuous now. I needed to borrow some money from Danny.

I'm not taking any risks, he assured me. Why should I? It's just a job. I don't even know who owns the place. If they come through that door, I'm not going to stand in their way. No chance. This hotel up in Belfast . . . they just handed a bag to the man and told him to leave it in the toilet and go home. Why should I try to do anything about it? They can blow up the whole town for all I care. What's it ever done for me?

I was laughing through all this, which only made Danny more annoyed. He thought it was important to convince me that he wasn't a coward if he didn't do everything in his power to safeguard the building.

I don't even know who owns the place, he told me again. Nobody does. Nobody knows who owns anything. They take their chances and build a hotel; that's not my fault, is it, if the ceasefire breaks down? That's business, isn't it? What do they expect? I'm not going to risk my neck for their investments. They don't give two shites about me. I wouldn't mind but the money's hardly anything to inspire acts of heroism. And the manager goes to me as he's leaving, looking down

61

his nose at me: You know there's a lot of people relying on you; this town's got to look forward into the future.

I was breathless with laughter by this stage, leaning on the counter in the overheated lobby.

And look at those old photos, he said, indicating the black and white scenes of Derry streets in the early 1900s. They're depressing the hell out of me. You start to see them all moving about when you're here long enough. I've started to dream about them as well. You see that one of Shipquay Street, them all parading about in their big dresses and top hats . . . that's the worst one. That's the one I'm going to smash. I'm standing in here all night on my own with them. I bet they never even bloody existed. They're just fakes or something to make us believe something. Would there be a reason for that, do you think?

All his talking put into my head that he was trying to avoid something: So how's Noreen? I asked him.

It's all sorted out.

He shrugged and went back to keeping his eye on the door.

If I tell you to duck, he added, get down behind the counter just in case it's one of the guests. There's only about five of them. Journalists probably.

You don't seem too bothered.

They keep the whole thing going. Parasites.

I mean, Noreen.

I am so, he said with an offended air. It's all sorted out. We went out for a drink and talked it through. What do you want me to do? Jump up and down?

And the two of you are back together?

He nodded, without looking at me.

It's all on again? Engaged as well?

He shrugged this time: I suppose so.

I reminded myself that I was there to ask him for a loan, so I had to be careful what I said, so as not to upset him. Although it was obvious he couldn't leave the hotel, I tried to persuade him to come for a drink with me.

I'm sick of that room, Danny. And I'm broke anyway. But

I'm not signing on. Some girl you used to finger up a back lane twenty years ago and having to ask her for money, through a sheet of bullet-proof glass.

Irritated, Danny said: It's not hers, is it? Take what you can get . . . So what are you going to do, then?

About what?

He shrugged and went across the lobby again to check the street. As he came back towards me, with his hands in his pockets and his head bowed to avoid my eyes, I thought he was a coward. He was ill at ease and wanted rid of me.

Knowing it would annoy him, I started to tell Danny about the purifier: I saw this thing the other night up the Culmore Road and it keeps going round in my head. I don't know what it means. But it's important; I know it is. It means something. At the old church hall. You know the steps? A crowd of alcos must sleep around there. I'm watching this man –

I was interrupted by the sight of a girl over Danny's shoulder, her face pressed to the glass door, who was mouthing some words to me.

She was American; she had cropped brown hair (cut by her own hand to save money, although she stayed in expensive hotels); she had short legs and broad low hips like a gunslinger; her face was pretty but gaunt; she had shaved off her eyebrows; under her university sweater it was clear to see she was flat-chested. I put my arm around her and kissed her neck.

Within minutes, the girl had told us her life story – a series of schools and then university, the death of her boyfriend in a car crash while he was on his way to her apartment for a birthday meal, and how her parents and relations had clubbed together to fund a trip around the world that they hoped would help her forget. She listed the cities she had visited: Paris, Prague, Rome, New Delhi, Singapore, Oslo, St Petersburg and now Derry because of her grandfather (who was an Irishman, she admitted with a full blush). Now she was tired, she said, and wanted to go to bed. Once she had apologized formally for her garrulousness, she offered me her lips and stepped into the lift, where she waved vigorously to us as she waited for the doors to close.

She told us about her life with the untroubled air of someone who has accepted that it is all entirely meaningless.

Without asking for the loan from Danny, I left the hotel. The night was mild and dry; I decided to take a walk out to the Line, the old courting path along the river bank where solitary men lit fires and fished or watched the army hiding in the reeds on the other side, and sometimes a crowd would form and the drink would be sent for. On the way through the Bogside, I met Quigley and a few others, who I knew slightly from years before. They could see I was at a loose end and enticed me into a night of joints and videos. Waking up on Quigley's sofa much later, I heard dogs barking and sirens and the noise of a crowd like drowning far away, and then silence, and then a helicopter thundered past over the roof. I walked back to my flat in my bare feet, but the city was quiet.

5

I woke up early the next morning, and waited for the lull after the workers found their holes. I got out of bed and sat in my chair by the window. The morning was wet and dim so I switched on the lamp sellotaped to the wall. My neck ached; I knew I had slept badly, out of reach of dreams. I wanted a glass of water to clear my throat but I kept putting it off for another few minutes.

Through a window across the street, I watched a woman washing up in her kitchen. She wore a yellow towel wrapped around her head like a turban. An old man waited for his dog to take a piss against a tree; he was someone I thought I remembered from my childhood, perhaps to do with the IRA, because I looked at him with a mixture of fear and excitement and then pity got the better of me. The dog shivered in a gust of wind. A dull mist, or a cloud of smoke, hindered my view of the river and the dismantled cranes on the docks.

I asked myself what I wanted to do that day and when nothing came to mind I made a plan to have a shower, get dressed, and go out to buy a paper. I could read it in the café at the corner where the waitress knew my face by now. Although I smiled at her each time I went in, she neither looked nor spoke to me more than was necessary. In quiet periods, she often sat at one of the tables with a man who had a terrified look about him, wide-eyed and unshaven in a dirty suit, rolling cigarettes in his trembling hands. He seemed to relax when she slid in beside him. One day she painted her nails while she talked to him; he watched her with a degree of wonder that made me jealous. I often wished I could hear some of their conversations.

My window needed to be washed. I yawned and thought about going back to bed. The street remained empty for a long time. Then behind the bushes of a house up the street, I spotted a soldier on his knees, with the gun close to his camouflaged face. After a few minutes, he jumped over the bush and took up a position behind a parked car farther down the road. In the meantime, another soldier occupied his place behind the bushes. Three of them made their way down the street like this; there would be three more on my side of the street.

When they were gone, it struck me that there were green buds along the branches of the tree. I needed to do some laundry but I pushed it out of my mind. I let my eyes close and began to think about Italy. I had lived there for more than two years, almost all of that time with Valeria. It was her birthday not long before I left; we went for a meal and danced a little. I wasn't sure but I suspected that it was the same night that I had slept with her friend Agnes, who lived in the same building. Valeria always fell asleep as soon as we had made love, and often I would go back out into one of the local bars.

The woman who had been washing up earlier appeared at the front door in her coat, looked at the sky, and went back inside for her umbrella. As she was locking the front door, a car stopped in the street. After some hesitation she walked towards the driver's window and leaned down with a surprising elegance that made me think of my childhood again, and the time I had run away. As I watched her giving directions to the driver, who I couldn't see, I tried to remember what had happened and where I had run to but nothing came back to me – only waiting for the cathedral doors to open in the early morning, and the dejection at finding that the radiators were still too cold to touch.

The woman laughed and touched the buttons on her coat. As the car made its way down the street, she put up her umbrella. It was a windy day, the cloud remained unbroken but the rain was a little way off, I thought. My feet were getting cold but I didn't move to look for some socks to put on.

By lunchtime the cloud had darkened, and there had been a shower of rain. The racket of the plastic sheeting on the house next door was making me restless. The Spanish students below were having lunch together like they did every day; despite myself, I envied them their laughter. I felt the desire to sit still and not do anything. I was hungry but it would mean going out. I tried to think some more about Valeria, and why I had left. Instead I found myself trying to piece together my time in London: the stoned days in cafés in Islington, collecting my dole every other Thursday, writing the book of stories in the squat, then leaving for Spain with the money from selling it. None of this held my attention for long, however; I kept returning to the image of the purifier and his lone fastidiousness and the puddles of beer from the empty cans. I had a cramp in my stomach thinking about why he had done that.

The rain didn't stop all afternoon. Nothing moved on the street but the cars and then groups of children once school was finished. An hour or so later the buses went by full of teenagers behind steamed-up windows. I must have missed the woman coming home; I caught sight of her again in what was probably her bedroom, looking directly at me through the curtains. My light was on so she could see me

66

better than I could see her; I waved to her and the curtains closed.

As soon as it was dusk, I picked up a book and started reading, but it bored me and I threw it on the bed. The street lights had come on. I tried to fall asleep in the chair. My mind was uncomfortably blank. Getting out of the chair, I started to pace the room, touching the wall on either side of my bed. I thought about writing a letter to somebody. My reflection seemed to grow clearer and more compelling each time I passed along the bottom of the bed, in front of the window. My hair was standing up and I needed a shave. I was losing weight. The people on the other side of the street would think I was on the dole, or a lazy student, and a lonely one.

I sat back in the chair. Couples went along the street between eight and nine. Then towards midnight I heard shouts, laughter and sirens. I drank some water, went to bed and must have fallen asleep immediately.

The next three days went by like that; I didn't stir from the flat. Lorna found me in a seedy torpor when she knocked on my door one afternoon – she pounded on the door with her fists like she had done that first morning in the dark. My first thought on hearing the knock was that Martina had come with bad news. For a few moments, before I hauled myself out of the chair, I was plunged into the scene of my mother's funeral, halted for some reason on the broken cobbles of a back street in the lashing rain, and I rested my cheek against the side of the coffin, my brother in front of me supporting another corner, a long high wall painted with a mural, and the mongrel seagulls broke into a frenzy of screeching in the trees as if they knew before I did that I was going to drop it.

Lorna was bleeding from her head. She had been on a demo in the city which had turned violent; she needed to find somebody to blame for this. Out of breath and unable to stand still, she continually touched her wound and cursed. I paid her scant attention; it was obvious to me she was delighted with herself and wanted me to witness her euphoria. She went over the same description again and again of the long moment of lamenting stillness before the first outburst of disorder. A stone or a flying placard had struck her on the head, she told me, and before she knew what she was doing, she was running for her life. She felt stupid now for panicking and wished she had stayed on to see what had happened. She was lucky to have run past my door or she might never have stopped, she claimed.

I'm calming down now. Do you want to go back with me to see what's going on?

I refused. Later, I found out the trouble that day was nothing more than a brief scuffle at the back of the crowd.

The idea of the demo was to put pressure on the unions, Lorna explained to me impatiently. They've been silent now for twenty years or more. Even after Bloody Sunday. Do you realize they are the biggest political group in the North, and they spend all their time scared of doing anything political? She gave me an incredulous look that made the blood on her face seem painted on. Why aren't the unions sitting at any talks table? These are the workers' unions, the workers' representatives. They haven't said a word about the end of the ceasefire. Why do they never say anything and no one asks why not?

Although she had hardly crossed my mind since the argument with the speaker, I wondered why I wasn't surprised to see her. Nevertheless, I said: I didn't expect you to call.

But did you want me to?

Ignoring this, I told her I had nothing to stop the bleeding and left it to her to make up her own mind whether to stay or leave. It made no difference to me at the time.

She sat on the floor opposite me, a pot of tea and cups between us. We drank the tea in silence and gazed out the window, at the rooftops drying after a shower. Intermittently, when the cloud broke, a small light flickered nervously on the window ledge like a young wet bird. I knew Lorna was trying to convince herself that it was all right to sit in silence together.

She got to her feet, her jewellery rattling, and mimed an interest in something out of the window – as soon as I was safely looking the other way, she rushed across the room in the other direction. She had the remains of my bottle of whiskey with her when she sat down again which she poured into the teacups. She had washed the blood from her face and taken off her denim jacket.

Some days there's no hope for us, she said cheerfully.

She was clumsy and heavy and she smuggled herself around in loose skirts and coats and big jewellery. The clamour of her jewellery was a distraction from her unwieldiness but also an absurd slapstick accompaniment. As I got to know her better, I realized that she suffered acute embarrassment when she had to move around in front of people, in a café or a bar, without some way of diverting their attention, without the cloak of her coat. She hated summer viciously: she was dead by the summer. In her flat or my bedsit, if she had to cross the room to get something or to pull the curtains for me at dusk, she would find some ruse to draw away my attention, and then set off at a run. If I happened to catch her in flight, she instinctively raised herself up on tiptoes; I watched her make tea on tiptoe, carry a plate to the table and take a shower on tiptoe. She rarely went up to the bar.

After a taste of whiskey, she said to me: I did you a drawing. Of your dream. The one with the children . . . and the bonfire. The feast.

Her face showed enormous surprise that she was telling me this.

It's the first thing I've tried in ages – in years to be honest. It's just a charcoal sketch. Are you still having it?

I shook my head.

What's wrong, Niall? she said, suddenly. Can we just start from here? I'm sorry about the other night, OK? You were right; we were ganging up on you.

Maybe you weren't, I said to confuse her.

She shut her eyes in frustration. Does it matter?

I don't remember it.

What do you remember, Niall? she asked me with overbearing earnestness. Tell me.

I felt disgusted: I thought about throwing her out but I knew I didn't have the energy.

Nothing. And nobody. Nothing and nowhere, I shouted at her.

She stared back at me.

Do you want me to go?

I made a scornful laugh.

Very crafty.

What is? I don't understand. What is?

You know what I'm talking about. The way you're asking me if I want you to go.

She frowned and closed her eyes again and then drank some whiskey.

Do you? she said.

I said nothing. It was her choice.

We finished the rest of the bottle without a word. She took out her earrings (bronzed shells) and placed them on top of her hair clip on the window ledge. A rainbow struggled feebly into existence above the river, faded and reappeared again with a blast of vibrancy. I heard her gasp but she kept her words to herself.

She went out to buy another bottle. I was able to forget about her completely while she was away; I felt queasy and miserable. When she came back, she complained that I was looking at her as though she was a stranger. In an awkward and overlong ceremony, shaking her hips and pouting ineffectually, she slowly peeled back the brown paper bag around the whiskey.

. . . I just gave it up. The eighties in Belfast were . . . What were you supposed to paint? For who? Your own nightmares. In blood? For who? I couldn't find a form – no, that's too pretentious. Look at what Duchamp said, or Max Ernst – no, that's not what I mean. I couldn't do it, that's all. I was mediocre, no more than that. All I could do was paint my own nightmares. Sheer utter stomach-turning self-indulgence.

She was telling me again why she had given up painting.

We were both drunk by this stage, scornful and dogmatic. Lorna was sitting in the chair, facing away from me towards the window; she had taken off her boots and placed them neatly in the corner; she sat with her legs folded under her. The trees along the street were filling up with birds as the afternoon began to thicken and blur.

So you've just been sitting here for days, you said? Did you see anything interesting?

As she asked this, her face seemed to seek some kind of mercy from me.

Just me, I said with too much sarcasm.

She stared down into her lap. She had missed some blood on her earlobe.

So anyway, she went on suddenly, breathing in as though she was gathering her courage . . . then my nightmares started to get the better of me. They took me over completely, all right. They just grew and grew. Then it was like they were just too big for me – they were too big . . . like I couldn't support them, three separate ones. They were outside of me in the world. I used to sit at the window and watch them coming down the street with the old women . . . like wee clouds above them . . . or bits of rubbish, old bags blowing about – that's more like it, bits of rubbish. What do you think of what I'm saying?

She caught me unawares: What do you mean?

Are you laughing at me? You are, aren't you?

Leave me alone. I'm doing my best, I told her.

She stared at me for a while and then held out her cup for more whiskey, and smiled warmly.

So I had a bit of a bad period . . . round the bend and round it again, she tapped her head. A bit of a bad period . . .

Hospital?

Near enough. My boyfriend Phil wasn't cut out to be a nurse, you see. He left the country to get away from me, you know? He moved to London. Imagine being the cause of somebody moving to London! She laughed unpleasantly at herself.

I saw her reach down for the whiskey bottle and then raise it over her head.

Do you dare me?

What?

Like in that awful story of yours. After they find him in the wardrobe.

She widened her eyes and tilted her head coquettishly. My only reaction to this drunken revelation that she had got her hands on my book was to sneer.

Still with the bottle over her head, she sneered back at me: I make a fool of myself every time I come here. Do you not think I know that? Do you? Do you want to hear what I was thinking in the shop?

I want the bottle, I said, sprawled on the floor at the bottom of the bed.

Do you know why I came round here that last night late? Do you want to hear?

She poured a little of the whiskey on her wound; she hissed between her teeth. The whiskey ran down each side of her face and met at her throat.

I came round because one of the nightmares had come back. That's why I came round. OK? The worst one, the queen. I'm in this big house, and they're all coming in to say how happy they are for me and – do you think I enjoy humiliating myself?

She was crying, her face creased up with self-disgust.

It's no wonder. Listen to this, then, she said, snarling and slurring her words. I was coming home the other night, and there was this gang of wains, ten-year-olds, coming towards me . . . and they all started spitting on me as . . . they took one look at me and they all started spitting on me – all over me, in my face and my hair and I just stood there and didn't say a word. I couldn't move. It wasn't shock. I just stood there dead still and them all spitting and slabbering on me . . . this woman had to come over and help me.

While she was saying this, I moved towards her and put my hands on her breasts – her tears dripped down on the back of my hands, some of them yellowed with whiskey.

There I'm telling you everything now, she moaned.

She shut her eyes as I opened her shirt. It was dusk now. I heard the plastic tarpaulin slapping in a fitful wind.

They were just wains, I tried to comfort her. They were just picking on you because they knew you wouldn't fight back.

Why'd they know that? she cried out loudly. How could they tell?

She pulled me against her and started to kiss me. I saw a tiny fissure of greed in her moist eyes that then sealed over.

I was skin and bones next to this deadweight woman. She undressed herself in the darkest corner. Her body was broad and cold and lonely; she reminded me of a terrible night I spent following a snowplough down the avenues of a city whose name I didn't know. There was an oppressive calm to our touching that was sorrowful and unclean; we struggled wearily to forget ourselves.

I am sure I was crying in her arms in that bed. The two of us perhaps, swamped by melancholy. I had the feeling she was a long way away, looking on sadly at the untemptable anonymity of her own body, her immoral distance from her own desire. Each breast to me was the like the belly of a dead pup. Lying on top of her, I thought I was going to cry out for forgiveness, or vomit. Then she held me in her arms, sunk in an atrocious musk of gloom; my heart shrank and died away within me.

PART FOUR

1

I slept through the days usually. The few times I forced myself out into the streets on a jittery *passagio*, I walked around in a daze until, in the lunchtime crowds or stopping suddenly on a mouldy back street, it was alarmingly plain to me that I had to get back to my room as quickly as possible or I would collapse at somebody's feet, jabbering nonsense. Behind the curtains, the whelping twilight whispered about spells and sacrifices to my blood.

Lorna listened to me in the evenings while I got drunk in her kitchen. She never tried to comfort me; sternly, in the candlelight, she questioned me and made me repeat the details of some story as though she refused to believe my explanations for what had happened to me, or she hoped I was lying. Perhaps she thought I was making fun of her. She placated herself with the idea that I was hiding vital information about myself, that if she was patient I would eventually tell her everything.

You're the one who says nothing. It's me who does all the talking, I pointed out to her.

Is that right? she said, filling my glass with wine. She gave me a look of mock astonishment. My constant drunkenness was unmentionable – she knew she had to deny me the satisfaction of being accused of having no respect for her.

Why're you not with anybody, then? I accosted her. You're thirty-two, you've a career. A lot of women would be married. You're alone. Your only friends are . . . in the party. Who's the last person you went out with?

I don't think it's right to talk about people like that, she said, on the verge of laughter, covering her mouth. (She was wearing a black velvet top that revealed her shaven armpit when she raised her arm.)

Like what? I don't want to know what they were like in bed.

Don't talk like that. She tried to look offended.

Don't get me drunk, then.

Why do you want to know, anyway?

You're the one claiming I can't just go on running from everything and rejecting everything. Where's all the wonderful things you've embraced? Where's your *joie de vivre*? You rent a wee house with a girl who's away off to India and you're sitting here. Why didn't you go with her?

To India?

It doesn't matter. Anywhere, I said. No, forget it. Get back to the question: who was the last person you went out with? Describe him.

I will not. She got up and opened the kitchen window and we heard nothing from the night and the air was damp and old and skulked on the floor like a sick animal.

Was he a teacher? I went on. What happened? Did you disagree over politics? Or couldn't he make you come?

Stop it, Niall? she asked me in a gentle voice. Don't talk like that. It's only a pose anyway. You don't believe it.

Don't I?

She was leaning against the sink, her arms folded under her slovenly breasts, her head framed in the black window.

Describe someone you know to me, then. Describe your mother, she said, smiling at her own craftiness.

Mad, I said.

Lorna continued as though she hadn't heard me, frowning and then smiling: You see, some things are . . . I don't know. If somebody asked me to describe my mother . . . I wouldn't be able to do it. It'd be like I was betraying her.

Only because you're ashamed of her.

I am not, she said, startled by the accusation.

You're too afraid to admit it.

You're obsessed with shame, that's your problem, she leaned forward and said into my face. You're ashamed of yourself. You're eaten up with it. You're ashamed of the fact that you're even sitting here with me. Aren't you?

Her eyes filled with tears – an entreaty not far from madness.

Aren't you? Tell me you're not.

I lost myself in a strange dread before the savage humility in her eyes. I did not think even to try to answer.

She went out of the kitchen, without slamming the door, and left me alone with the smoking joss stick and the candles she painted on with black ink.

2

We could do with another Night of the Bad Meat . . . but for women this time, the fat one said to me after drawing my attention to the ugliness of the girl behind the bar. She was thin with a small bitter mouth and a brittle hunched back.

I forced a wink of understanding.

So did you think the foreign women were much different, then?

He didn't give me time to answer.

I was in the States for two years, you know? I was seeing this Brazilian one. You should have seen the state of her. Well over the top. Wigs and huge cleavage and false eyelashes and boots up to her thighs.

He scrutinized my face for a sign of our mutual understanding.

How much?

He tightened his eyes at me, pursing his thick wet lips: I was right, I knew I was. I know where you're coming from, don't I? We've the same taste. You can have a ball to yourself here, you know. Derry's a dirty hole.

Another one wanted to talk to me about London: he thought it was overrated. The loudest of them assumed that I had come back because I was full up with stories – the only point of any experience beyond lying in bed was to stand in the bar and tell it on, and there were only so many stories a man could carry around without unburdening himself. The one in the suit with the ponytail wanted my opinion on the way the Derry was starting to look like a placeless suburban cul-de-sac.

The pub had a wooden floor and artificial black beams overhead. Every conceivable object was hanging from the beams: pitchforks, boxing gloves, an oil lamp, a stuffed fox nailed up by the tail, a small ladder, dried flowers, a sewing machine, and rusting wing mirrors from old cars. We were out early, about ten of us, celebrating a birthday; it was somebody Danny knew.

Although we had nothing in common, each of them took it in turns to draw me into their talk; they were high spirited and generous, and dangerously obsequious. Danny kept checking if I was all right while he regaled me with tales of their drunken antics that he thought would amuse and impress me. I cursed myself for failing to escape my miserable state of mind. My silence began to embarrass everyone. In the toilet, where I went to hide, I stuck my fingers down my throat.

Later, back amongst them, I noticed a girl of about eighteen gaping at me; she was dark and slight but with large breasts she strained under. Her hair was outgrown and tousled like a boy's, and her arms were bare. She had delicate, undecorated hands. She never smiled.

I touched her hair before I even spoke to her. I couldn't take my eyes off her; she resisted my gaze with ingenuous dignity. Then she would glance at me, embarrassed and begging me to leave her alone.

I can't, were the first words I said to her.

Right in front of me, her brown eyes sweetened with melancholy. She was light enough to lift with one hand.

Come outside, I commanded her.

Silently, she asked me again to let her go, her face bewildered and plaintive. She followed me into the street after a few minutes.

I have to touch you, I told her. She squeezed my hand and looked away as though I was saying goodbye to her.

Danny put his head out and called me into the doorway. He wanted to warn me to take it easy on her; she was the younger sister of the friend who was having the birthday. He also hinted that the girl had very little experience of men. Her parents had once taken her to see a priest because she was so quiet.

Back on the street, I immediately asked her to kiss me. Shocked, she stammered that she was too young for me. Her wet petrified eyes never left my face. She was trembling. We stared zealously at each other for a long time. People going in and out of the pub noticed us. She didn't know how to conceal her emotions.

My tongue dried up; I began to sweat. With great caution, I lifted my hand to her breasts but she moved out of my reach, blinking and trying to get her bearings.

Let me touch you. I have to.

Why? she asked gravely.

I have to.

Why? she begged to know.

My head was spinning as though I was completely drunk.

She set off unsteadily along the street, her arms out in front of her . . . Catching her up, I pushed her into a shop doorway where she suddenly clung to me. She was shaking convulsively.

What are we going to do? she sobbed into my ear.

I knew the situation was in danger of getting out of control.

Let me feel your breasts, I said.

Will we stop then? She looked into my face with a trusting serenity.

I promise.

Do you? She put one of her fingers to my mouth – my lips were stuck to my teeth and tasted of puke.

After a decent interval, I returned to the pub. She was in the toilet. Danny saw how drunk and restless I was; he put his arm around my neck and, winking blatantly, introduced me to a red-haired woman who he then left me alone with.

Look after him for me. He likes to think he's dangerous, Danny said to her loud enough for me to hear.

The woman and I failed to interest each other in the slightest and soon we were arguing about something to hide our awkwardness. The bar was much busier now, lots of girls in pairs with too much make-up. My hands had grown numb as though pins and needles were about to start; I had already suffered through them on my face, while the redhead talked to me about a play she had a role in. It's nothing to do with politics, she was at pains to have me understand. Above our heads, the strung-up objects hung in the smoke and the shadows like carcasses being drained in a slaughterhouse. All I could think of was the young girl's startled, curdled eyes as she looked down at me sucking her breasts in the doorway. The redhead, noticing my distraction and the way I couldn't keep still or look at her, began to talk proudly about her capacity for intimidating the men she came into contact with. The fat face of Danny's friend, sweaty and hiccuping, inspected me over the shoulder of another girl; he nodded eagerly to me to tell me that he thought I was on with the redhead. The rest of them were deciding on a club over the border or one of their houses.

I must have passed out. When I came round, sitting on the street against the wall of the pub, Danny was standing guard over me. The ground reeked of pigeons and old beer. Danny was listening to another man who was talking at a frantic pace, gesticulating angrily at himself and everyone passing – then some people stopped and Danny had to intervene. While this was going on, I got back on my feet with the idea of making a run for it.

Where is she? I demanded of Danny a while later. He had started walking without a word to me. We were on a street of new redbrick houses, garden walls and bay windows.

She's away home, he told me sourly.

Where? Do you see what I mean, Danny? She's beautiful. Do you see what I mean?

Danny leaned against a wall and spat between his feet: You should have seen the state of her. She hit her head off the cistern.

She fell?

She was banging her head against the cistern like . . . whatever the fuck you want.

Banging her head? I shouted.

What the fuck did you say to her? Danny shouted back to me. I told you, didn't I? She's not well.

He was knocking his head with his knuckle. She's sick.

Nothing. I don't know, Danny, I swear, I tried to convince him, grasping for his hands. I had started sobbing and couldn't stop – I was practically laughing because I couldn't stop. Danny kept his eyes averted, staring up the street along the pale curves of clean kerbstones in the new street lights.

Do whatever the fuck you want, Niall . . . but you're carrying on the right way to get your head punched in.

He sang mournfully as we walked back to his place, his parents' house where two of his brothers still lived also. We sat in the front room eating toast with his mother, who fell asleep in front of us. Danny teased the bottle of vodka out of her hand and pitched it at me to finish off if I wanted. The room was dark and dented like an old box. Nothing had changed since the last time I had sat in there, maybe ten years earlier. I didn't understand why he was making us sit along with his mother. No matter what I tried to talk to him about, Danny was set on silence, a plate of crusts on his knees.

His father, a tall, gaunt-faced man, came in from the next room; I was the only one to make a greeting.

You been out? the father asked his son.

It was a great laugh, Danny said.

I wasn't sure if they were joking with each other.

Ma's asleep there, Danny added.

The father stared at the rubbish stuffed into the fireplace for another minute. He shrugged at something.

The town's busy, I threw in.

The father glanced at me sharply as though he had not noticed me before. Then he went on into the kitchen where the light stayed out and he didn't make a sound and he stayed just long enough to be forgotten.

On his way back through the living room, he stopped again, a can of stout in his hand.

Was it a good night, then? he asked.

I expected Danny to give another dry response but he merely grunted and threw a crust into the fireplace.

As soon as the door was shut, I started laughing – I was waiting for Danny to laugh as well.

You two would keep the town up all night, I joked.

Danny reacted with instant vehemence: Who are you to talk? Your brother threw you out sure.

Are you all right? I asked him, taken aback.

Why?

You don't look it.

He opened his mouth to speak but it turned into a convoluted shrug.

What's the matter with you?

Fuck all, he said, irritated.

There is.

Is there? In a quiet, monotone voice, looking straight at his mother in the chair, he said then: We don't all have to blabber everything out to everybody.

Is that right?

He nodded slowly.

And that's what's the matter, is it?

He shrugged again.

I fell silent and we went back to watching the television or his snoring mother or the uncurtained window with the mildewed piece of cardboard taped over a hole in the glass. Before long, I stood up to leave.

Are you going? He seemed surprised.

At the front door he struggled with how to say that I could stay if I wanted. Inexplicably, I felt sorry for him. He snorted mockingly to himself as I gave him my excuses for why I had to go.

A helicopter was out. Danny struck me as sickly and depressed; I found it painful even to look at him. After the gloom of the house, I was relieved to get back out into the air and the night streets. The frail young girl in the pub, the bruised forehead and the changeful murky eyes under the mop of boyish hair – the desire for her that had choked me to the point of blindness was already dead.

3

Lorna sat on the bed beside me as I tried to talk my way out of the feeling that I was losing my mind. In only an old T-shirt, she leaned back against her pillows, her arms folded under her loose breasts, as though she had made up her mind not to touch me. She had washed her hair earlier that evening, which made it double in bulk. With a vexed frown, she asked me outright why I had left Valeria; she had asked me the same question on a previous night.

There was no point any more, I told her. Valeria knew what was happening but she could block it all out of her mind. When I look back on it, I was happy there for a long time, more than I've been anywhere.

Something must have happened, Niall. Things don't change for no reason.

I told you. She found out I was sleeping with her friend. But it wasn't that. She would have forgiven me. She would forgive me anything to preserve her peace of mind. I was growing sick of myself.

So you left to protect her? Lorna asked optimistically.

I don't know why. Anything I say, I don't really believe it, Lorna.

You were honest with yourself. Some time apart will be good for you.

That's totally wrong, I cried, losing all patience with her attempt to see my actions in a benevolent light. Listen: there was this Spanish lad I met once while I was travelling around. He just came up to me one day in Barcelona and gave me some bread. He hadn't a word of English or me of Spanish. He was living on the street but he was always spot-

85

less, and neat and elegant. We rarely tried to speak but we travelled around together – he'd go off on his own and come back with wine and food for us.

I don't understand, Lorna slapped the duvet suddenly. What were you doing living on the street?

That's where I wanted to be.

What did you hope to achieve by that?

Not a thing. Callously, I was enjoying her incomprehension.

So you were pretending to be down and out? You were just travelling, really?

I wasn't pretending at all. I wanted to let myself fall. I thought you would hit some kind of bottom eventually and stop . . . that you could only go so far down. But there is no bottom and . . .

But you must have known that, Lorna rebuked me. Anybody could have told you that.

I resented her complacent tone. She was too busy trying to catch me out to listen.

Why did you think there should be a bottom? She sneered at the idea.

It was absurd but I thought the world wouldn't let people sink that low. I trusted people.

That was only partially true, but it was enough to embarrass her.

Anyway, at the time, I'd no appetite for anything except my own destruction, I said after a heavy silence. Her face showed extreme pain.

I went on: The Spanish lad. We drifted about together. This was in northern Spain and France. After I left London. One morning – we spent the night under a slide in a children's park – I woke up and knew straight away that I was heading off on my own. I can't explain why. I was standing looking at him and he opened his eyes. He knew as well. He put out his hand and we shook and I went. No discussion and no reasons.

Why are you telling me this? Lorna covered her face.

86

Then in Toulouse, listen, about a month later. I'd been going around on my own, losing interest and fed up, thinking of going back. Outside the train station, this Muslim man is swiping at me with a knife –

Why? Lorna shrieked.

He'd bought me something to eat and thought he owned me. Then the Spanish lad just appears between us. Well dressed, graceful, clean. And he stands between us . . . and takes the knife in his heart. I just ran –

You did not. Lorna sat forward in disbelief.

I had to. What would I have said to the police? I never even knew his name.

I can't believe that, Lorna said and covered her face for a moment. Then: You see? There must be something good in you to attract that kind of person.

I laughed. Don't romanticize it, Lorna. There was no big force pushing him on to the end of that blade. Just his own will, impeccable, aimless. He stuck his perfect nose in without being asked.

Lorna tried to change tack: What's this got to do with you and Valeria? That's what I've been sitting here wondering. I don't know what you're talking about at all. Try to be a bit clearer, will you?

I can't remember.

I knew this would get at her but the connection between the story and Valeria had actually slipped my mind.

You should go back to her, she said then.

I was sure Lorna meant this purely as an incitement to my pride. She looked at me to show she was serious. In defiance, I took a letter from Valeria out of my pocket and handed it to her. She refused to touch it; when she saw me opening the letter, she got off the bed and begged me not to read it.

La vista di me che soffro ti annoia, I said again and again. Do you know what that means? She's saying that her tears bore me. She found me in the gutter. Of course her tears bore me (I was shouting now) because they bore her. She wants to see me fall again . . . *Perché non riesci a trovare pace a casa?* Why

87

can't you find any peace at home? She knows better than me why I'm back.

What does she know? Lorna snapped.

She wants me to drag her down because she doesn't want to do it herself, I went on ranting. She wants to cry tears that don't bore her. She wants my pain. She doesn't have any of her own – she doesn't have any pain of her own.

Lorna made a face to show she thought I was talking nonsense. Then: If you believed that you wouldn't have stayed with her.

She hurried out of the room into the kitchen where I heard her fill the kettle with water.

I read some more of the letter aloud: *Tu sbuffi come un uomo sotto la pioggia, con un lungo cammino davanti a sé.*

I had no idea what I was saying any more. One thing made as much sense to me as another. The sound of Lorna opening cupboards and handling cups and cutlery was as unbearable as – her sanctimonious indifference would drive me to do something stupid and spiteful.

I threw myself off the bed and headed for the front door . . . She came running after me, but without losing her self-consciousness, pulling down her T-shirt.

I'm going.

Why? she asked with genuine confusion. Is it me?

I didn't know how to answer this; privately, I knew that I wanted an excuse not to have to sleep with her.

You can't go. You'll end up . . . she sighed dramatically. It's my fault; I'm cold, aren't I? I'm no help to you. I'm a selfish . . . Go if you want.

Leaning against the wall, she slid to the floor, where she sat with her head on her knees and the charred ribbons of her hair touching her toes; she was wearing a thin silver toe ring.

How are the dreams? I asked her, without knowing why. Are you still having them? Worse?

With a movement of her head, she let me know she was. Then she told me how that day in class she had heard a noise in the corridor like footsteps on gravel and she had gone cold and begun to shake with horror; her students had noticed and gathered round to comfort her.

Why? Why? Look at what you're making me do – I shouldn't be telling you all these things, she said and apologized immediately. Wiping her eyes, she stood up and pulled off her T-shirt; she was completely naked now in her hallway.

She kept her eyes closed, her face behind her hair.

I need you to stay, she said in a cold, desultory voice.

I followed her into the bedroom, managing to avoid seeing her from the back. To my dismay, she undressed me frantically. I was too weak to put a stop to it. She sat on top of me; I shut my eyes but nothing came to life in the darkness. She put all of herself into kissing me as passionately as she could.

4

The next morning I persuaded her to take the day off work. This trivial act of disobedience put her into an overexcited and whimsical mood. I lay in the bed watching her get dressed until she broke down into a fit of giggling and ran into the bathroom. With her short arms and ugly back, her shyness was a hopeless melodramatic fake. I entertained myself with the idea that she found me just as unattractive, and where this might lead. Her room was stuffy and chaotic; books and papers and dirty clothes filled an armchair, boxes torn open, sacks of ornaments and old jewellery and there were cobwebs in every corner.

The light that morning had the sweetness and grievance of spring in it. We were going to find somewhere to eat breakfast. She hooked her arm in mine as we walked into the city centre; she smiled at people she knew and stopped to talk to a man wheeling a pram. The streets were dusty and faded and without ancestry.

None of the pubs had opened their doors. A security guard waved to Lorna from the foyer of the supermarket; he was an ex-boyfriend of her sister from years before and was always asking for news, as though there was still some hope, she told me when we were out of sight.

You're done for now. I tried to make fun of her: It'll be all over the town. You're supposed to be in bed sick anyway.

People have more to think about, she said, but before I could tell her what I thought of that sentiment, someone tapped her on the shoulder.

She let go of my arm as she introduced me to him: a young man with a bleached-white skinhead and deliberately camp gestures. They talked for a few minutes about a meeting that evening, and then about a woman walking past, who blessed herself as a joke at the sight of us standing there and looked at her watch.

Has the big day come? she called back.

You never know, Lorna shouted after her.

Well, I'm away to the doctor's for my dose of happiness. Give me a shout when the looting starts.

We were amidst the market stalls in the shadow of the old city walls. She introduced me to another man selling leather belts – the smell of leather hung in the air under the vault-like arch. Another stall had keyrings and calendars that featured copies of wall murals and photographs of the street fighting in the 1980s. Lorna acted appalled, although she must have seen this stall every morning.

Look. You can buy the memorabilia already. It's terrible. I don't know whether to laugh or cry. It's only a few years ago. Look at how quickly capitalism stops us having any relationship with the past. It's completely meaningless . . . already.

I wasn't in the mood to argue; I had a luxurious erection. A gull cried out from the sky. At another stall two tourists were trying on Celtic jewellery. The big hewn stones in the walls would never get any light on one side, I was thinking. Lorna had her back to me as she rummaged through the articles on the stall, her broad hips in a velvet skirt slightly worn across her buttocks. She was arguing with the stall owner, a squat red-faced man with an overgrown moustache, who I could tell was prolonging the argument so he could continue eyeing her cleavage, which would come into view each time she reached across the stall for another knick-knack that aroused her anger.

As though I was moving closer to give her my support, I put my arms around her and brought my groin against her buttocks. Lorna responded by arguing more vigorously. With as much restraint as I could manage, I began to press myself against her; I wasn't sure that I wanted to come, just to bring my senses to a pitch of pleasure. At the same time I kept my eye on the stall-holder, who I hoped would catch on to what was happening – he took a drink from a can of beer and winked at me.

Lorna, perhaps unconsciously, pushed her hips back against me as though enjoying the pressure from behind. With my fingers I felt the line of her underwear around her hips, and plucked it. Absent-mindedly, while he was pointing out to Lorna that he had been in prison, the clown-faced man turned his head and spat over his shoulder and the slabber hit the wall with the sound of a kiss and hung there on a disfigured mossy stone.

Forgetting myself for an instant, I put my mouth to Lorna's ear and asked if she wanted me to come. The gull was crying again over the city. Lorna nodded in assent but then stopped mid-sentence. Spinning around, she studied my face in desperation like a woman searching for a clue about how to escape.

Despising her cowardice, I said: What the hell do you want from me?

A number of emotions passed across her face before she came up with an answer: Niall? What's wrong?

You are.

Her eyes greedily consumed the repugnance on my face.

We were having a good time. Weren't we? What's wrong?

In the hope of avoiding an argument at any cost, she was willing to forget what I had said to her and what I was doing while she was remonstrating with the grinning stall-holder who was now scratching his own groin.

I grabbed her by the shoulders. You make me feel mad and cheap. Nothing else could do that this morning but you. Your shock sickens me. Who are you to be shocked? Shyness won't protect you. Your opprobrium is as futile and crafty as all those trinkets you're complaining about. I don't even care whether you exist or not.

I was making no sense to her or myself. She stared at me like I was insane.

My groin was hurting me as I walked away. Hearing the noise of her jewellery behind me, I turned round in a flash of cruelty to catch her running the last few steps towards me; her breasts juddered separately, her elbows were pinned to her sides and she had her eyes closed like she was going to run right past me, and never stop.

Perhaps she didn't want to die alone. Perhaps she felt she didn't have the strength to make it as far as her own death. When she wavered or fell, she hoped I would help her back on her feet to finish the journey. It surprises me how few people decide to abandon this world hand in hand, in a fit of mockery or joy. We are deluded by the idea that death must be a solitary experience at all costs. Why do we think it is courageous to meet our death alone and in silence? Imagine instead the frenzied carousing of another naked horde as they dance their way towards the red heart of the abyss. She used to say that I thought death wasn't good enough for me.

We ended up in a pub that had just opened. When I had heard her talking about the meeting that evening, I toyed with the idea of getting her so drunk she would be incapable of making it across the city. After a couple of hours' drinking, her naive delight in spending an afternoon in a dark pub was making my skin crawl and I wanted her to make it to the meeting so that she could make a fool of herself. The people at the other tables were having lunch.

I could get used to this, you know? Skiving off work and telling the day to get lost. Is this what you do every day?

Only when I've things to do.

And after all that we didn't even have any breakfast, she laughed at us. Are you hungry? I'm starving.

I put my hand on her thigh; the touch of velvet sent a shiver through me. Little by little, I dragged the skirt up her legs while I asked her questions about the meeting.

I'm supposed to be speaking tonight, she confessed suddenly.

What about?

It's my own idea, she said. (The skirt was at knee level now.) About drugs. Not just E or coke or – prescription drugs. The doctors keep this city going, you know. The men all die young and the women go to the doctor. The whole city's on a wave of Prozac, everybody I know's on it. We're all drugged to the eyeballs. An acceptable level of intoxication. Direct rule by chemists.

She leaned forward and kissed me on the cheek – it was a sign that I should stop tugging at her skirt.

You sound like a nationalist, I said, pretending not to understand.

I am. The British administration should not be allowed to portray themselves as neutral arbiters between warring tribes. I can't believe I ran after you, she said then.

She stared in the direction of the barman who was talking with some men in suits at the bar. The tips of my fingers touched her cold skin.

You know I don't think I've ever run after anyone in my life before. Maybe that's why I did it? she said brightly. To see what it felt like. I can't turn up drunk. They'll all know.

It'll be good for them, I said and slid my hand between her thighs. You're all too serious. Why does protest have to look like misery?

You're hardly the life and soul of the town, she gasped on the last word. Don't, Niall. Not here.

No one can see. I want to make you come.

No, she said and kissed me again nervously. Why, anyway?

I got my fingers inside her knickers and felt her hair; she was brittle and dry.

93

Forcefully, she pushed my hand away. Why here so much? I'm not an exhibitionist, you know.

I was unable to speak; I was doing all in my power to control my frustration. I brought my finger to my nostrils and smelled it – leather, her soap, stout, and then offered it to her.

I've had enough of this, she said, keeping her voice down. She made moves to stand up and leave. She was pale, harassed.

Does that disgust you?

It doesn't appeal to me, she said with prim formality.

I laughed. What does appeal to you? You're always cold. You never let go.

She thought for a minute, one arm in the sleeve of her denim jacket: You've no idea how much I'm trying, she said quietly.

Do I need to be more patient? Can't you have an orgasm until the workers seize power?

I was sunk in a state of sordid malevolence that no amount of talking would lift me out of.

Let's go home. She tried to take both my hands. Just not here, Niall. We'll go back to mine.

The tenderness she summoned into her turgid haunted face – I wanted to take out my cock and piss on her. Luckily, the barman approached to collect our empty glasses and asked if we wanted another one. Lorna shook her head but I said yes and ordered some whiskey with it. She sank back on the bench; we were sitting on a kind of raised dais with a large gilded mirror behind us. As long as she kept silent and ignored me, I would be able to control myself. The barman returned with my pint and short.

Am I boring because I don't want to have a . . . in a pub?

I grabbed her hand and put it on my groin; I couldn't think about anything else but one of us coming.

What the hell is wrong with you? she shouted at me and covered her face.

You can't even say the word, I scoffed back at her, enjoying her outrage. The barman was studying us.

94

Why are you behaving like this? You're trying to shock me. You are, aren't you?

I ignored her. Then I felt her hand on me again.

Right you asked for it. She hid her pain with a nonchalant smile. In silence, with increasing determination, she rubbed at my cock but she couldn't make me come – she lacked any skill in what she was doing. After much too long, she gave up. The atmosphere grew more despairing between us; we should have separated at that point without another word.

To escape, I went to the toilet and wanked myself but there was not much relief when I finally got it out of me. I hoped I would open the door and see that she was gone but she was sitting there, sipping another half pint of cider.

What are we doing? she asked me then. We're wasting our time, aren't we? Hurting each other.

I decided not to answer her; the cramp on my spirits was worsening.

Just go home, Lorna. I'm better on my own for the minute, I managed to say to her.

I'm not leaving it like this.

Just go home, Lorna. Leave me alone.

No, she said, taking another drink.

A silence grew up between us and then absorbed us until we were lost in it, suffocated and insignificant; not even an act of absurdity could have freed us – the very possibility of an absurd gesture was unimaginable (to jump up on the table and sing an Italian folk song). In the doleful light, Lorna twisted the rings on her fingers and scowled at a dried quiff of wheat stuck to the wall. A young boy rushed through the swing doors, took a look around for somebody and left again, with a salute to the barman. Shadows passed along the street on the other side of the stained, glass windows. At one of the big tavern tables in the centre of the bar a couple laughed in unison as they looked through some photographs.

None of this could have been any different and yet it was all a sham – with a fraught grip on the table, I was on the point of screaming or vomiting at the sense that everything was somehow absolutely mandatory, and yet at the same time it was all part of a vast impersonation. The purpose of this stage show was beyond my comprehension, unless it was that the material world itself relied for its existence and nourishment upon the intrinsically evil essence of illusion. When the memory of the purifier returned to me on top of all this, as though there was a link between them, I jumped up from the table in fear, unable to take any more of my own mind – for I saw myself down on my knees in front of the purifier, sucking his cock.

To distract myself, I went up to the bar to order another drink, without asking Lorna. The barman, chewing his lips, listened to me with the contempt of a priest. I warned myself that I was being paranoid. His arms were completely decorated with tattoos. Another man across the bar, a drunk with a bruised face, wiped his mouth on his sleeve and was about to speak to me. I was in a cold sweat, knowing there was violence in the air. Glancing across at the bar at Lorna, who was putting up her hair – she was as ugly and graceless and virtuous as the city she was dying in.

I said to the barman I was going out to buy some cigarettes but he insisted he had every brand behind the counter. I told him then that I wanted a newspaper and he asked which one for he had any I could think of.

I want some air, I said too loudly.

You get some air, he replied in what I thought was an ominous way.

What?

You want some air, he said my own words back to me, showing me a gold tooth.

As I left the place, the drunk was calling a warning to me. After a few steps, I found myself running in a state of nameless, swelling panic. The light was fading around me, sucked up from the streets while everyone pretended not to notice. People's faces and voices seemed to get in my way as I ran, more than their bodies or their shopping bags. I felt the pres-

ence of horror that savoured its own futility in the over-
bright shop windows, in the children playing in the twilight
square, in the gloomy battlements and the sight of the crowded escalators in the shopping centre. A dog, a ragged mongrel, ran at my heels, not barking or snapping, running along
beside me as though he knew where I was going.

5

I knew I could not possibly love her. If I have to say that I
wanted anything from her other than her company through a
time when a sullen and overblown anguish took control over
my life – I was intrigued by her ugliness. Her ungainly
wretchedness gave me some relief from the torment in my
mind.

Would she be alive now if I had loved her? My life is not
any more worthwhile for knowing her. Or remembering her.
The thought of trying to save her never entered my head. She
may have wanted a witness to the implacable approach of
her own death. But why did she choose someone like me,
who wouldn't be trusted? She must have known that I would
make an incompetent witness. I can't explain what I was
doing there in that city with her; I stutter and exaggerate and
make a meal out of the simplest of facts; I appear cold to the
point of brutality; they would bring up irrational incidents
from my past that would undermine my credibility. I wasn't
really paying attention during that time. Why should I have
been?

Perhaps, when she began to realize that she would not be
shown any mercy, when she accepted that there was nothing
she could do to avoid that sudden misguided spray of bullets, she felt ashamed of herself, like every victim, and desperately hoped that I would be her alibi.

One day I saw her coming towards me down a street on the
outskirts of the city. Even though I was certain she had seen

me, I ducked through a gate and hid in some bushes. She gave nothing away when I talked to her later that day, even when I lost all patience and blurted out that I had seen her. I accused her of lying but she insisted she hadn't noticed me; the argument grew more ferocious until she finally confessed that she had spotted me. I wonder now if that confession was untrue.

6

The morning had passed without me leaving my chair by the window. I was afraid to move, shivering with a gross unrequitable expectation. The cathedral bells rang for a wedding, while a man I thought I knew from school brushed the street. As long as I didn't panic or jump to any conclusions, I had the feeling that I was on the brink of being rewarded by some revelation. The day was formless and cold, as if the wind had brought smoke with it. Below me, the students must have opened a window because I could hear them talking and then a little later the sound of a Spanish ballad.

Hours of lavish anticipation when anything seems possible. The streets lead the way towards a tender and devastating brink. The eye empties itself into the new world's exorbitance. Violence sweetens the air. I have never been able to understand these moods, which come sporadically and unbidden. Nothing ever comes in the end. I am left exhausted and disillusioned, cursing myself for being kidded again.

The streets were no comfort when I went out. As usual, because there was nothing else to do, I went into a pub. In secret, I pleaded with the world to offer me a way out of myself other than the excess of a baneful concupiscence. The daytime drinkers were somewhere else that afternoon – every bar I tried was lonely and dark.

I went up the steps on to the city walls and walked towards the army observation post. A cold, irritating mizzle began to fall. The pebble-dashed Creggan estates on the hills were hidden by cloud. Rosemount, where I was born, was blocked from view by the cathedral spire. Unable to find any relief wherever I turned, I walked back towards the city centre with its new multi-storey car parks and shops and hotels, back above the Guildhall Square where I had first seen Lorna. The big river was tired and dirty. A helicopter was landing in the Waterside. Under a low grey sky, the city cowered between the empty hills, morose and scathing – it left me feeling rankled as though the city had been built with the deepest reluctance, with strange qualms and fears, to spite its own heart.

A minute later I was rushing back to my flat, compelled by another surge of anticipation that took me by surprise; I was sure I was going to begin some writing. At the time, I was unable to think about how long it had been since I had written more than a few lines, which I generally threw away, but it must have been nearly a year; the last time would have been the poem I wrote for Valeria while we were in Sicily, at the pink house on the cliffs.

I ran into Martina and Louise on the Strand Road but made up some excuse for why I couldn't stop, doing my best to appear cheerful and in control; she said she wanted to talk to me and I promised I would see her during the week. When I got back to my room, I lay down on my stomach on the bed, a position that helps me calm down. I stayed like that for a long time. The urgent sore gaiety gradually drained away, no matter what I did to try to hold on to it. Letting the spittle build up between my lips, and drop of its own accord to the page, I watched the paper turn to mush. It was dusk again. I shut my eyes and prayed for sleep as the only way to get me beyond that moment.

Later that evening, I went for a meal at Lorna's. Danny was there also. They both did their best to ignore me, which I was glad about. We were drinking wine. Lorna wore a black satin dress with a sagging cleavage. Her mouth was painted red. There were small scarlet flowers in her long earlobes. Neither

Danny nor I had thought to dress up. Her resolve not to let us see her disappointment sparked off my bitterest desires; I pictured taking her roughly and against her will, a dark filthy cellar, bloodstained walls and the keys rattling on my belt.

An hour must have gone by while I listened to them talking, mainly about people they knew in common and times in the past, and drank glass after glass of wine; I ate almost nothing. Lorna put on some music when she took the plates away. She said there was dessert but it was forgotten in the end. The music was unknown to me but I didn't ask. Danny was in talkative form, with elaborate questions for Lorna which I was sure he had prepared and learned off – each of these questions could have been asked with nervous sincerity or sarcasm.

Socialism tells people what's good for them, doesn't it? Is that a stupid question or not? Danny put his elbows on the table and shook his head in confusion.

For the first time that evening, I succeeded in laughing.

Not stupid . . . Lorna said, not stupid but . . .

Look at Derry, he went on, as though the thought had just occurred to him. Everybody's better off now than a few years ago, more jobs, better houses, shops – that's right, isn't it? Cars and TVs and all the new shops – people have more money. The ceasefire's ended . . . but there'll be another one. But the socialists think it's all a bribe, don't they? Bad money. But why shouldn't we take it if it makes our lives better? Why should we be the ones to be any different, bribes for peace or not? We're not special. Do you see what I'm getting at? . . . Am I missing the point, do you think?

What's the Night of the Bad Meat? I interrupted before Lorna could answer.

That's just a story, she said with a wave of her hand, hoping to resume the debate as quickly as possible. Her eagerness for this kind of rational argument infuriated me.

I know some people that swear they saw it, Danny disagreed quietly, as though he was talking only to himself.

The night they killed all the dogs? Lorna asked him.

100

Danny nodded and shrugged at the same time: The Brits. That's what I heard, anyway. The dogs were like an early warning system. You see, if a Brit came within smelling distance of the Bogside, or the Creggan, the dogs started barking . . . so they could never spring any surprises. Our dog died, anyway.

My Da killed ours, I threw in.

I heard all that was just a myth. Lorna remained adamant.

They scattered poison meat all over the Bogside, over into the back yards and the lanes. In the morning, the people made a pile of the carcasses in the street, hundreds of dogs you're talking. And set a light to it.

That couldn't be true. I grew up in the Bog. I would have remembered something like that, Lorna said. The Brits had their own dogs; one of them was knighted sure – a bomb-disposal dog, I heard. They probably had undercover dogs working in the Bogside, she laughed and clapped her hands at her own idea. She was getting drunk; her face and neck were reddening.

Danny shrugged again and turned to me with a sly gleam in his eye: Talking of stories – I was thinking about you the other day, the time you were in London. All those stories you were telling the English ones about growing up in the wars. You never saw anything. A bit of broken glass maybe.

I laughed, slightly embarrassed: It's what they wanted to hear. At the start, I told them I knew nothing about it but they thought I was just being nice.

And you see when the IRA started bombing England, they were all over the moon. They would have given a hand if they'd been asked, Danny said, looking at Lorna in disbelief.

Lorna took my hand under the table and asked Danny to tell her more about what I was like in London.

There was a whole pile of them, he said. A house of drop-outs. Hippies and punks and – none of them did anything. A big squat with about ten rooms in it. It was like a train station but nobody was going anywhere. And there's me over looking for a job. No one had any money. They were bloody tapping off me for fags. They'd all gather in the big room and plot the revolution at night.

Did they now? Lorna squealed with laughter and dug her painted nails into my palm.

And him there sitting in the middle of them trying to philosophize and going on about plastic bullets and riots and imperialism.

Revolution? Lorna raised her eyebrows and smiled; her eyes were moist and dilated.

Then I wised up, I said back.

So is that who the stories are about? The people in the house? It sounds like them.

That's why I had to leave, I lied. They were all after me.

So do you not want to write about here? she asked me then, with a slight slur in her voice. About Derry? I think the dog story would be a good one . . . So who are you trying to write for anyway?

She was leaning on her elbow, sleepily, dazed with pleasure at the simplicity of her question. Releasing her hand from mine, I glared at her to say that I didn't want to talk about it, but she deliberately ignored me.

Who do you want to read your – ?

Shut up, Lorna. Danny, how's the fiancée?

Don't start on me. He held up his hand and gave me a side look that I didn't understand. I was drunk now as well and convinced that Lorna wanted to make a fool of me in front of him.

All of sudden, I was raving: What the fuck would you write about, anyway? That it's a dead-end and it rains a lot? That a balaclava is as hard to find as a good blow-job?

But don't you feel any responsibility? Lorna stayed calm, smiling almost tenderly at my outburst.

I wanted to hit her.

You can't just forget about the world outside of yourself, Niall. That would be –

Responsibility for what? This place did nothing for me. All it did was to leave me feeling guilty if I wanted anything more than misery and a few pints. Like a lot of people, I was only born the day I left here. On a ferry on a rainy night, squeezed between two slot machines.

Lorna yawned: Is this the hedonistic position again? That's how far your analysis has got, is it? That capitalism gives people more freedom to have a laugh? How many people, I wonder? How many people live in poverty to support the few having a laugh?

How many people want everyone else to be miserable and bored and bitter just because they are? I argued back weakly in a low, mean voice. Danny, do you know she's having dreams that she's going to die?

So am I, said Danny. Big vivid ones right this minute.

Lorna burst out laughing and then so did I and the laughter grew more uncontrollable when Danny, who was also drunk now, ran into the middle of the room and did a comic version of some song in Irish, rubbing his hands on his trousers and spluttering like a horny ageing pederast; he knew exactly what each of us would find funny. He wanted me to go up next but I refused all their pleas. Lorna didn't wait to be asked; with one hand on the back of the chair and the other holding on to her hair, she recited a Yeats poem:

> Foul goat-head, brutal arm appear
> Belly, shoulder, bum
> Flash fishlike; nymphs and satyrs
> Copulate in the foam.

I was appalled, speechless. She was sniggering with her hand over her mouth but it was impossible to tell whether she meant to be grotesque or not. Danny whistled, his fingers in his wine-stained mouth. Lorna's slovenly scarlet face, her pale thick pimply arms, and the spots of food on the front of her dress – her vision was blurred and I expected her to be sick at any moment. I went into the kitchen to get away from the sight of her.

Before I knew it, I had come back into the room where she

was stumbling about with a CD in her hand and said: That was the most obscene thing I've ever . . . You're bluffing, aren't you?

Come off it, Niall, Danny intervened.

She stood with her big back to us. Slowly, she turned round and looked at me, trying to control her sniggering: You think you can't get a blow-job here? Listen to this, then: I was in Belfast with Phil . . . and we were out one night. Just in a pub, just me and him. But these two fellas started on him outside. Phil was lying on the ground and they were kicking him. I was trying to stop them. He was unconscious and bleeding. But what could I do? Me? Then one of them took out his cock in front of me.

You're talking shit? I shouted at her.

He did. He took out his cock and said he'd leave Phil alone if I . . . did it.

A lewd ridiculous grin came across her face; she could have been on the verge of tears.

Danny laughed.

So I did, she said and hiccuped. And there you go. And guess what? I had to do the two of them.

You're making it up, I said.

And guess what? When I told Phil, do you know what he did? Guess? He punched me. I had a black eye for two weeks.

She came back to the table and finished off the wine in her glass. Danny asked her if she was all right. She gave the impression that she didn't know where she was. I was unable to go near her.

Danny left shortly afterwards. With only a word, I would have gone with him. Lorna was lying face down on her bed in the dark when I went into the room a number of hours later. I sat beside her and unzipped the back of her dress; her skin was damp and cold but lacked smoothness in places. She was awake. I massaged her arse under her dress while she wept.

What's the matter with me, Niall? Whatever I do, I make a mess of it . . . I'm so scared all the time.

Our sex that night was morbid and violent. Her eyes rolled in her head; I thought she was losing control, finally, but a moment later she screamed in rage and pounded my face with her fists. The loneliness that drove me towards her – it was barely an echo in the haunted cavern of her life. My come froze into stalactites inside her.

Afterwards, we were despondent, aching with failure. We turned away from one other in mutual abhorrence. Each time I closed my eyes, I was met by images of violence and destruction that made me too afraid to consider leaving. Our lust tempted us with visions of light and salvation that stayed perpetually beyond our grasp. We grappled and sweated for a way out of ourselves in vain.

Why should I continue with this? None of it made any sense to me at the time. Some days the absurdity of my life managed to dress itself up in the guise of solemnity. I am not writing this for her sake, as a memorial. Or for my own diversion – just to be rid of her. I ask myself now what I know about her, the facts of the case. She was thirty-two, two years older than me. Her dreams overflowed into the world. She studied in Belfast where she fell in love (her very words) and became engaged to a man who left when she had a nervous breakdown. At night, if she was alone, she drank spicy red wine. As a child, she was regularly taken to see her father in hospital while he lay in a coma after falling from a scaffold (she was the only one there when he woke up). She threw a bottle of milk at the army one misty morning on her way to school. She lost her virginity in an amusement arcade. When I gave her a book by Genet, she dreamed that her photograph was stuck to the back of his cell door in a collage of blank-eyed pouting gangsters. There was an older sister living in the south of England, married with two children, who wanted to forget where she came from, and a brother in Australia. A cousin was serving time in the Maze. Outside of the Party, she had no friends. She suffered fits of guilt about being a teacher (the quiet hand of the state, she called herself in these moods). Her mother stayed up late into the night knitting and humming to herself. She liked the smell of lemon and broke an egg into her thick black hair once a month. She learned to drive very young. She believed in God; one night when I found her crying in the back yard, she told me that she wanted to pray but she was afraid of what might happen. She wore big clothes to hide her heftiness. Chapel bells, rabbits, nursery rhymes, soup, parks – these things she hated. Against her will (for she thought it conflicted with her socialism) she was fascinated by early abstract art. Her father was a recluse. Other than a brief attempt to move to London, she had never been out of the country, although she talked about Berlin as though she had lived there – the sun was her enemy. She was at her best around seven in the evening. She couldn't sing or dance. For no reason she ever tried to explain, she practised small acts of self-denial, blushing when I caught her at it. She liked me to whisper in her ear. She cried a lot. She wore too much moribund jewellery. She didn't love me. She laughed like a disappointed prostitute. She knew she was going to die.

PART FIVE

1

It was the hour of the day when the city seemed deserted. A crowd of people, maybe fifteen of us, walked in drunken procession through the empty streets in the bad light of dusk. Some corners and doorways and lanes were already dark. A girl was singing at the front, a bitter whining song without a refrain; somebody beat softly on a bodhrán at random intervals. Lorna held my hand and laid her head on my shoulder. Everyone had been drinking; the stillness of the town humbled some and inspired the rest to run riot.

I must have slept for days. Danny reminded me where I was supposed to be when I encountered him on the street; he had come looking for me on Lorna's behalf, angry at my lack of consideration for her. I was only out of bed; I was supposed to be with her at the graveside of her friend who had killed himself. It was a Sunday, hollow and uneasy. Without going home to change my clothes, I went with Danny to The Lesson. The dead man's girlfriend had a superb white neck, long, thin, unbending – like a punishment.

Lorna was maudlin and abusive; she was drinking heavily, whatever was put into her hand. She accused a number of people to their faces of being hypocrites and not giving a damn about her friend's death. As soon as we got to the house I tried to shake her off, but she turned up wherever I went, looking forlornly over a shoulder at me or standing in a window, with a condemning snarl. To wake her out of this spell of resentment, I broke a glass in her hand. Some people went to her aid and took her out of the room; she gazed back at me placidly, almost voluptuously.

After that, I forgot her. Most of those in the dead man's house were strangers to me. People were coming and going all the time. I followed the girl with the classical neck from

109

one group to another but she always found some excuse to ignore me. I was too far gone to know whether the others noticed my behaviour, getting drunker and more stoned – everyone was. There were people dancing in a room with canvases stacked along the unplastered walls. A tall woman in a black Spanish shawl and a turn in her eye told me an incoherent story about the dead man and a night in Galway when he stole a boat. She didn't miss a breath when I kissed her bare wrinkled shoulder.

I've just kissed you, I said into her ear.

Have you?

I'll have to do it harder then.

Whatever you like, she said, shrugging her shoulder near my face. Her dress smelled of seaweed.

She agreed to dance with me; then someone turned the music off in protest at the dancing and I lost her in the confusion. While everyone was arguing, Danny came to get me with the news that Lorna was making a spectacle of herself in the kitchen.

I know what's wrong with you, she growled, pointing at me as soon as I came through the door. Don't I? I know all right.

I cleared the people out. She refused to sit down; she was marching around the kitchen, bumping into the table and walls, scolding herself, mimicking herself, her face streaked with black lines. I had never seen her so agitated, even when she appeared at my door in flight from her dreams.

What's the matter with you? Look at the state of you, I pointed at her now. The sight of her sobered me up immediately.

A friend of mine crawls under his bed and dies, that's what's wrong with me, she screamed back. I can't get it out of my mind. Is that so mad? I don't want to have a good time. Crawling under the bed like an animal . . . lying on his back under the springs. And how did she find him, that girlfriend of his? How did she think to look under the bed? Would you look under the bed for somebody? Would you?

She was determined to get an answer out of me.

Are you trying to say she knew what he was planning?

Maybe he wasn't planning anything, she wagged her finger shakily at me. She blinked her eyes to keep them in focus. He would have told me. He wouldn't have done it. I saw him a few weeks ago. He was . . .

She leaned against the fridge, her voice sank to a whisper: I've been so selfish lately. Caught up in myself. I've been so –

You couldn't have stopped him, Lorna.

You know what he said to me one time? We were coming home one night and he stopped and he just put his foot through a shop window. The alarm went off but he wouldn't move. He kept saying it over and over again: Some of us don't stand a chance. And we know who we are. We notice each other on the street . . . and we lower our eyes. We're not made to survive.

Although she was drunk, she spoke those words like they were burning her tongue.

I heard he was a junkie, I said, resisting the temptation to argue with her.

He was not. He pretended to be so people wouldn't ask anything of him. That girl of his: would she have stayed around for long? You can see it in her eyes. Pure scorn and –

Stop going on about the girl. Do you think she murdered him, then? Is that what you're trying to say?

Jim was –

Maybe he was just sick and tired of himself. The dark and the wildness. The failure of every attempt to get outside himself, no transcendence . . . no raptures . . . no transgression . . . no –

What are you talking about? she shouted at me with shocking force. I sat down on one of the chairs at the table, losing all pretence of being clear-headed.

I'm not feeling well, I said. Remember I told you about the man emptying out the beer cans? On some steps?

No. You didn't tell me that.

I did, I shouted back at her. I don't care, anyway. I ended

up sleeping there the other night, you know. You wake up and you're lying on these old steps that stink of piss and . . . there's an old coat under your head and –

What were you doing that for? she said in a shrill, alarmed voice.

How do I know? I must be sick or –

You must know. Don't you remember?

Saying nothing, I glared at her murderously – this woman who was desperate to believe that life is under our control, that it is inherently meaningful and directed towards the good.

She screamed at me again: Stop it. Stop looking at me like that. Stop trying to frighten me.

You scare me . . . with your tactlessness. You can't even manage to have a fit without worrying if it makes sense.

At least I'm not fake, she came back at me, her face bloated and raw. I'm not a hypocrite. You're just a bastard, aren't you? A coward.

She started laughing to herself, stumbling around the kitchen again, picking up empty bottles and cans that I thought she might throw at me to prove she could act on a whim.

And you didn't answer my question. Her voice was slurred again. I stayed silent.

Just answer yes or no. No discussion. And you have to promise never to ask anybody the same question. So promise.

I nodded sadly.

Imagine there's a gas, a harmless gas, right? And you can release this harmless gas out into world . . . and everybody will be happy. So happy. Happy as . . . she shrugged. A gas. Do you press the button or not? That's the question.

I took my time, unsure whether I was thinking or merely pretending. Lorna folded her arms and steadied herself by resting against the sink which was full of dishes. One of her eyelids was almost completely down.

Do you understand the –

112

Yes, I answered.

She nodded in an exaggerated way as though I had given her the answer she had expected.

I'd hit the button even if it wasn't harmless. If there was only a few of us who could live to our full potential. No matter what. Do you hear me?

Her face tightened into a drunken sneer: You think you would . . . but you couldn't. You wouldn't be able to. You'd go mad. You can't take away from people . . .

I didn't want to think about her ruthless question any longer. Her other eye was closing. She was babbling nonsense.

You should go home, I told her.

Can't you stand the sight of me any more? she smirked. Don't leave me. Oh, please don't leave me. I'll die, I'll fall away and die.

She was putting on an upper-class English accent. I stood up and kicked my chair towards her. Please don't leave me, she simpered and giggled to herself. At the bottom of the stairs, she grabbed hold of me and begged me on her knees to take her home – she grinned and bowed to the people on the stairs who tried not to pay us any attention. I didn't have the stomach to look at her; all I did was shake my head hopelessly. Maybe three more times that evening, she tried to embarrass me by calling me a coward or a fake when there were others listening. I tried to put her out of mind, continued drinking. The dancing had begun again. Then I opened my eyes to see her blighted silhouette in the bedroom doorway, and there was another pink girl beside me on the bed.

Lorna took herself out into the night. Veering along the pavement, she bumped into a car, a boarded-up house and then a streetlight which had a length of skipping rope tied to it that she wanted to jump and grab for but knew she lacked the energy. She stuck out her tongue at the rope; it had been years since she had done that last. She wanted to do it again, but the childishness of it caused her a sharp pain in her heart. Music came

113

from Jim's house. She shut her eyes in an attempt to think about him, so that nothing else would get in the way, but the immensity of the darkness seemed to rush towards her and then reared up at the last minute like a wave, and became a wall of immaculate white skulls in front of her.

With a loud groan, she opened her eyes again and hurried along the street, her arms held out on either side to protect herself. She saw an old man's face at a crack in a curtain and she nearly stopped to stick out her tongue at him. The still night air was unbreathable with its mixture of river smells and rust and the sweet sorry spice of new leaves (which always reminded her of the taste of lipstick). When she reached the corner, the sight of the straight main road with its lights and shuttered shops and parked cars gave her hope. She stamped her boots firmly as she walked. The river was behind the derelict buildings on one side of her. Like a hideous rusting web, a long wire fence had trapped an assortment of plastic bags and rubbish – for the briefest moment she considered how it would look as a painting or sculpture symbolising the craven forces of capitalism. I don't have a clue anyway, she muttered disparagingly to herself. It might as well be a holy grotto with all the rags and ribbons fluttering of the sick and the dead. Phil always refused to let her burn candles in the house.

In the city centre she sat down on a bench outside a building site for a new hotel, scorning the voice in her head that warned her it wasn't safe, the streets were empty, she was drunk. The sleeping city climbed up the hill to the cathedral spire and the red light of the army surveillance mast. She wished she was near the sea. The sky was out of sight in the dark. She thought of the hawk that lived on the cathedral spire and the Sunday morning it had attacked her as she stepped into the sunshine after mass . . . and flown off screeching with a clump of her hair in its claws, and how her had mother slapped her on the face as though she was to blame . . . and her father with the other men smoking in front of the grotto, shielding their eyes like they were saluting as they looked up at the bird in admiration. Her neck was stiff for a week afterwards and there was scratch on her ear.

A taxi came out of a side street and slowed, and a man asked if she was all right; she knew his face. He said to mind herself and drove away. Then she remembered sitting on the edge of a big brown leather chair beside a hospital bed where her father had been in a coma for weeks; his hands lay on the folded white sheet, his fingers spread like claws as though he thought he was still falling, grey hairs on his knuckles. She glanced at his face. He was looking at her. There was more grey in his eyebrows. She had time to think about how people's hair and nails go on growing in their coffin before he winked at her and went back to sleep just as she heard the sound of her mother's heels coming back along the corridor.

A scuffling noise at her back made her stiffen with fear, but when she turned round there was nothing to be seen; she smiled bitterly at her own disappointment. Jim's face appeared before her in the road again, his eyes bulging and ravenous and white – she wasn't afraid of him. They would still be drinking themselves into a frenzy in his house. So many memories were flooding back to her that she wondered if she was going to die that night; she saw the newly painted Land-Rover pulling upside beside the bench at dawn, and a cop touching the bundle of her in her coat with the tip of his rifle. Then she laughed out loud at the thought that they might send a robot in first to check that she wasn't booby-trapped. Taking off her earrings, she held them in her hand and, simply because the idea came to her, she threw them high over her shoulder into the building site. Her head was pounding from all the drink. Go home, catch yourself on, she said to herself in a voice she didn't like. She got back on her feet and began to walk slowly down the middle of the silent road, along the broken white lines, suddenly engrossed in the meaning of a dream from the night before.

PART SIX

1

I heard nothing from Lorna the next day. I didn't think about the possibility that I might see her again. As soon as it was dark, I went out drinking alone.

In The Lesson, an uncle of mine was drinking at the bar. His beard was short and greying now, and covered most of the skin on his face. His sunglasses were big and gold-rimmed, hanging by a gold chain. He was always the kind of drinker who seemed to grow more placid as the night went on, more innocent and tender, who would be there to the very end, humming lightly to himself as his head filled up with uncalled-for notions and emptied just as quickly – like the bar around him, which he was only dimly aware of. When he shook my hand, I knew that he didn't recognize me. He lived alone in a caravan out near the convent, where the river crosses the border and heads in towards the city . . . and cuts through the city effortlessly and spills across another border before the sea.

He was my mother's youngest brother. He had done time for the IRA in the seventies and since his release had taken to his caravan and a soft-hearted but determined alcoholism. They called him Sunshine because of his sunglasses which he had worn ever since I could remember. I used to imagine his eyes had been transfigured by the resplendence of the firebomb he was sentenced for. The last time I had seen him was at a wedding, when he stood up to say a few words; everyone fell silent. The minutes passed but he hadn't made a sound, his hands planted on the table, staring down at his plate above which his black tie swung back and forth like a sad scorched pendulum. Eventually, someone had to whisper into his ear. Before he sat down, he bowed resignedly to the crowded pentagon of tables and sought their forgiveness for going on too much and getting carried away with himself. One time, a rumour went round that he had been spotted kissing a woman in a car park. He was known to stay in his caravan for months on end.

I bought him a drink. It was a simple small horseshoe bar but the variety of undersized doors created the sense of different rooms, for different kinds of drinker. There were no windows. Sunshine snapped his fingers, blew a paltry whistle through his hairy lips, and said: I knew I was going to forget it. I wrote it down to remind myself, even. Did you see it? That programme last night? The documentary? BBC2? I had it marked an'all. You wait all week for something, you get all worked up about it . . . and then what? You just forget all about it.

He scratched his beard.

I didn't see it, I told him.

It looked good. About this pagan festival in Spain where they drape all these snakes over the saints' statues. There was another one on there last week about the Laps up in Norway. They have this kind of singing with no words in it. But then there's all the ones you miss, he sighed.

His voice was deep and muffled; he was a much bigger man than I recalled.

Did you see the one about the ceasefire? I decided to put him on the spot.

He turned his head towards me, and my warped reflection in the glossy black mirrors on either side of his rugged nose. His hands tightened into fists on either side of the pint, then went limp. He sighed again: Every time I come in here somebody mentions another thing I've missed. That's what I mean about it – you have to pay close attention to the schedules. When I got the TV there last month, I thought the times were like the bus times and you just turn up and wait. But it's on the button they start. Right to the second. Exact and precise. What else is like that?

He was both aggrieved and impressed. From our stools, we watched a woman ordering a round at the other end of the bar, her hands joined, and her painted nails reflected on the copper surface of the bar. The evening came back to me that I had seen my Da chasing Sunshine down the street, firing cutlery after him. He had discovered Sunshine hiding in the shed in the back yard when he had come back unexpectedly from his Saturday night out, because the soldiers had raided the pub. Sunshine scrambled out the back door with the plate of food my Ma had made for him, as she did secretly every Saturday evening.

So what do you think about it anyway? The end of the ceasefire – will there be another one? I tried again.

Aye, I've heard ones going on about it, he said. Who knows?

About what?

What did you call it there?

Ceasefire?

Aye. That's what it was. A strange word . . . but there's stranger. Who knows?

Do you think there'll be another one?

Another one? He looked bewildered.

Aye. Talks. Negotiations.

He shook his head in weary confusion. Y'know last week there, I was listening to . . . who was it? Ah, it doesn't matter. This man anyway was telling me that Sinn Féin were a counter-insurgency group set up by the British government. And there was no such thing as the IRA. I was speechless, you know? He was trying to convince me.

What did you say?

It had nothing to do with me, Sunshine said defensively, and held out the palms of his hands, which were white and wrinkled like they had been in water for too long.

It's hard to keep up with what's happening, he sighed and took a long drink. This man was explaining it to me. I got the TV an'all but it just makes you think you don't know anything.

But you were in jail? How could he tell you there was no IRA and you were in jail?

Aye, I know. What you're saying sounds right. To me anyway. I could have said that to him, I suppose. But he looked so sure, you know. He seemed to know what he was talking about.

But that bomb of yours?

That's another thing. Sunshine nodded and stroked his beard. Aye, you're right. You're right.

And what about all the people that have died? Tell their families there's no IRA and see what they say.

You're right again.

He's talking rubbish. You can't let people walk all over you like that. You have to stand up for yourself and your beliefs.

Do you think so? He drummed his hairy fingers on the polished copper. He was saying it to more than me, you know. That it was all a conspiracy . . . Candy Kelly, that's who it was. He had passionate beliefs. You can't take that away from him or any man. There was no IRA and we'd all been had. Frenchie O'Connell went into him, fists flying, about this business of the . . . what did you call it?

Ceasefire?

Aye, that's the word. It's a rare word isn't it? A very military word . . . he said suspiciously.

You're not called criminals any more, I reassured him. That's what Bobby Sands died for, isn't it? And Patsy O'Hara. All of them. They weren't joking, were they? Don't forget them.

It was my turn now to be carried away. I forgot to even scoff at myself, vulgarly trying to encourage a Republican to hold on to his faith – someone like me who had left the country the first chance I got.

Sunshine blessed himself and shook his head.

I was just standing there, he said a moment later. They roped me into it. Candy was . . . he shrugged. Opposing points of view, that's the real issue.

Angrily, he took off his glasses; he had a black eye. He put the glasses away in his pocket and took them out again immediately and laid them on the bar – he flicked at them with his fingernails like he was playing with the lacquered fossil of some insect on the bar. I thought he was about to break down in tears or smash them. I put my hand on his arm when I couldn't think of what to say to cheer him up.

As though he had come to a long-awaited decision, Sunshine gave the bar a slap. At the very same moment, a man burst through the door and rushed to the bar beside us. He was tall and frantic, with an extremely small face. The barman gave him a whiskey and he knocked that back. He locked his hands behind his head as he spoke. His voice was high-pitched and grating.

I just turned the corner, he began, You know what's going to be there – the wee street, the main road, then a rusty gate . . . what's left of the docks and the river. But there was something else there this morning. You have to see it, Sunshine. This ship, a gigantic thing, moored with big white ropes. A milky-white mountain at the end of the wee street – that's what I thought to myself. Hundreds of tiny wee windows and flags. You should see the size of it. The deck is way above the roofs. Masts and everything completely white, every inch of it, Sunshine. Not a speck of dirt on it, not even from the water. It's as near beauty as you get. It's hard to even keep your eyes on it, y'know, it's that white.

Sunshine put his glasses on again and finished his pint while the other man began to tell us the same story again. A big crowd was gathering, he said. We waited for Sunshine to come back from the toilet; I had put my coat on.

You going to have a look? he asked me, astonished. He got back on his stool. Fair play to you, Michael.

Why? Are you not? I said, ignoring my brother's name.

Easy does it, he advised me with a warning finger. I'm going to have to think about it. Sighing for all the thinking he was going to have do now, he plucked at his beard and ordered another drink.

White ropes? Decks above the rooftops? Tell us about it again – it must be some sight. He turned his back on me to the other man.

123

On my way to the docks, I stopped in to see Danny. While he was telling me about the new guests, I began to think about the American girl who had offered us her life story so readily. She was in her room, drinking brandy, and packing. The tan lines across her body made me imagine that she was growing out of her own skin.

2

I'm going to come, she whispered to me. Keep talking.

We were in the hotel bar, which bothered Danny more than my raucous drunkenness. I had been talking wildly to the American girl for about an hour, about Italy, about my brother, the entranced teenager in the train corridor, as though I was on the brink of seeing where these things were leading me. Next, I moved on to Jim crawling under his bed. I brought myself to tears without trying.

Keep talking, she shivered. I'm coming. Keep talking . . . Just listening to you.

Upstairs in her room, she threw off her scruffy clothes and stood on the bed, bouncing and flailing her muscular arms. She wanted me to catch her and then hold her down. She had broad hips and a weak, boy's torso. Her nudity was shallow and lean and guiltless – the sight of her made me decide to keep my clothes on, and my boots. She stroked my head gently and screamed shrilly as she came. When we finally stopped that first night, she wiped herself and went back to her packing as though nothing much had happened. I was incapable of leaving her that night. Through her window I could see the lights of the cruise liner like a city far below.

The next morning I got on a bus with her to Dublin, with only the clothes on my back. We stayed in a bed and breakfast near the coast. Neither of us liked the city; she said it had the air of a place put away in the attic. One damp morning, I persuaded her to start a conversation with a girl who we saw lying on a park bench – a junkie, sores on her face, with filthy hair and clothes, no more than twenty. I watched them from behind a tree.

What did you talk about? I asked the American when we had started walking again. We were both soaked by the rain.

She told me about her life. It was so horrible, Niall; she patted her own heart. She hasn't seen her parents since she was nine. And she's a daughter of her own. She's been raped and beaten. Her boyfriend grassed her up to the police. She's probably got AIDS or hepatitis. What can you do? I gave her some money but I know she'll spend it on drugs.

Did you come?

She denied it absolutely, got upset with me and ran off under the dripping trees. The next day, on the cliffs over the bay, she confessed to me that she had become wet but stopped herself in time. She chewed on a wart on the knuckle of her thumb. At my insistence, she managed to delay her flight home for an extra day. Greedily, I seized the opportunity to play the part of the lover soon to be abandoned.

I don't know what I'm going to do when you leave.

You can go back to that girl you told me about. Lorna. She needs somebody.

We were resting after a walk, in the long grass at the edge of a cliff, watching a ferry pulling away from the port.

I can't help her, I said. She's too heavy for me. It's like she doesn't fit anywhere. Like she's too awkward . . . or too ripe – your fingers go right through her.

Just be kind to her.

She's gone off. There's a lethal misery in her. It's started to smell . . . ferment. She'll choke me.

She wouldn't do that on you. She's not cruel, is she?.

Or maybe I'm the one dragging her down. I feel like I'm betraying her even talking about her. I don't know what she wants from me.

She sounds very lonely, the American asserted as though it explained everything.

I laughed derisively and lay back in the grass.

She's too far removed from the world to be lonely, I went

on. She doesn't like me and that gratifies her. It proves something to her . . . or justifies her. She likes to pretend she's in love with it, all of it, the world, everybody. That it'll all be OK. She believes that. She has these bad dreams and gets scared she's going to die. She's so big and clumsy and it's just her way of halting everything and bringing it under her control. It's her who's the selfish one. There's more hate and anger in her than there is in me. All her socialist talk is just a way of making everybody feel as disappointed and unhappy as she is.

Keep talking, the American girl encouraged me, seating herself on top of me, her eyes half-closed, pressing herself against my groin. In her hand she held a flower, a few petals left to be plucked, her frail blue wrist wrapped in leather ties.

Can't you stay for another few days?

She grimaced, staving off her irritation: Keep talking, please.

Lorna has these nightmares. She knocks on my door in the middle of the night . . . and sits there in my room scared out of her wits. She thinks somebody is after her. Or she's in danger.

More, she gasped as the sun came out behind her. She arched her back, biting her lip, and pulled up her skirt.

I don't even want her. I'm not interested in her body – I've never seen her come. She doesn't seem to care. She's like a corpse some nights. I have to make up excuses not to go to bed with her. And she knows – she knows.

I paused.

More, please. Her lips moved silently, her tongue curled behind the white teeth. I looked with a strange sadness at her narrow weak chest where the nipples showed through her pale vest. Much of what I was saying about Lorna, I had not put any thought in to.

Maybe I pity her, I struggled on, letting the words come by themselves. But I don't think so. She keeps too many secrets. She frightens me, I think. She wants limits for everything. She's afraid to dance in case the ghosts come out of the ground. No matter how hard she tries, there's no sanctity about her . . . or modesty. You know she gave up painting because she thought it was coming alive on her. She's sucks the world up through her theories like a straw and . . .

The American shuddered briefly and opened her eyes, blinked, and gave me the sight of her shyest grin.

Scared for an instant, I shouted at her: I'm not getting stuck here. All those years away . . . and I end up in a bedsit in Derry – with nothing better to do than run my lips along the cracks in the mirror.

Everything will be fine, she laughed in commiseration, touching my lips with the flower. It always is.

I pushed her off me and got to my feet. I took out my prick with the idea of masturbating over her where she was lying in the grass but I lost the urge as suddenly as it had been born in me.

You look so unhappy, Niall.

I am. You've no idea. I need a way out of myself.

Here's a way.

From the grass, she stretched up her arm and tickled my prick with the little flower. As soon as I was hard again, she knelt up and began to suck me, touching herself at the same time – each time her lips reached the base of my cock she forced me to take one step back in the grass, so that when she finally let me come, one of my feet was dangling over the edge of the cliff and the rocks below and I was holding on to her hair for my life.

In the morning, she went to the airport alone. I had planned to lose myself in the pubs in Dublin for a couple of hours but I ended up in the bus station, shaking with fear and waiting for the first bus to take me back up to the North. I phoned Lorna from the bus station; I rang again and again, unnervingly convinced that she was at home and listening to the phone ringing in another room.

I was glad to wake up in Derry the following morning. In a café I set about the task of writing a letter to Valeria, warning her not to come; she had written again in reply to a telephone call I had made to her one night, although I couldn't remember it. She told me in the letter that during our conversation she had filled an entire notebook with her doodles and scribbles, which she reminded me I used to say were the shadows of her spoken words . . . like the flocks of birds above the old alleys of Rome – *l'ombra degli uccelli che volano nel ceilo.*

She claimed that I had accused her of driving me mad with her saintliness: *Allora mi chiami nel mezzo della notte . . . accusandomi di averti fatto impazzire con la mia santa e irritante generositá.*

I was reading parts of the letter to Martina, who had surprised me by tapping on the café window.

You said that to the poor girl? Martina said with badly feigned interest.

The thought of Valeria's acute beauty, poignant and obscurely threatening, on the Derry streets made me go cold with anxiety – it was unclear to me whether I was afraid for her safety or my own on those sardonic streets. Encountering her for the first time on a long flight of crumbling white steps in Rome, I turned away, hoping the vision would pass me by as quickly as possible – it was early morning, warm and airless, and I had not eaten for several days. She stopped beside me to enquire if I was feeling all right, and with unnatural slowness she tilted her head at my confusion like she was quietly falling into a dream. Her hand rested on my shoulder; I stared at the patch of sweat under her arm, longing to rub my nose in it.

I told all this to Martina, who wasn't listening to me; below the make-up, her skin was grey and her eyes bulged with weariness. She looked unwell enough to inspire thoughts that she had no right to be out on the streets. I was too afraid to ask her what was wrong, or about Michael. She began to turn over the pages of a newspaper when the silence began to grow out of our control.

After a while, she said: I'm just so tired. Louise has been waking up a lot with these bad dreams. Night sweats.

I was curious to know if Louise talked about them but Martina stabbed at a story in the newspaper and pushed it towards me to read. The speaker, Lorna's friend, had been found beaten unconscious and stripped of his clothes up a back lane; he was in hospital; a policeman guarded his door.

I took a walk around the city centre, fighting to rediscover the cheerfulness I had felt on waking up back in Derry. Nothing held my interest for long; all I seemed able to do was brood incessantly on my depression in that draughty barracks of a city. The American girl had slipped my mind completely. Passing the bus stop for the hospital, I had the absurd notion of going to visit the speaker, that it would help me in some way. A woman was waiting there also, with silent white-faced children. When she caught me staring at them, instead of an admonition to mind my own business, she shook her head condemningly over them. Losing no time, she approached and began to execrate them loudly for their muteness, their docility, the way they clung to each other. Their own mother's afraid of them, she said within the children's hearing. When the bus pulled in, I pretended I had been waiting on somebody to get off.

I started to head back to my bedsit, contrary to what I wanted. Every face that passed near me was sinister and resigned. I dreaded the scrupulous finality of the moment when I would shut the door behind me. This is how people feel when they decide to kill themselves, I was saying over and over again in my head as though I was trying to talk myself out a terrible gesture. Hurrying through the streets, I kept my eyes fixed on the ground in case I should meet a glance that was cornered and wild and covetous – like that of the two children at the bus stop.

The idea of seeing Lorna came to me outside the front door of my building and I almost ran the short distance to the college gates, although it was much too early for her to have finished teaching for the day. There was no doubt in my mind that if I went into my bedsit and shut my door, someone else would have to kick it open one morning: how long would I lie there before they made up their minds that something was wrong? Until a neighbour complained about the smell? Only when the black-backed gulls gathered on my windowsill and tapped all night with their beaks at the glass?

After a few hours of loitering outside the college, watching the girls and the ceremony of green or gunmetal grey Land-Rovers going in and out of the police station, Lorna had not appeared. When I got to her house, she was watching the news on the TV. A bomb had gone off in England, two in the North, and a man had been shot dead as he waited for a bus in Mitchelstown. Lorna lay on the sofa under a tartan blanket. She didn't attempt to speak to me; I paced the room.

I got my dole this morning. Come on, I'll take you out for a drink. I need to talk to somebody.

She continued watching the TV.

You look terrible. Why weren't you teaching? Are you sick?

Suddenly, I remembered about the speaker: So you're feeling guilty, is that it? You think it wouldn't have happened if you had more commitment and you weren't wasting your time with a –

With a what? she screeched at me when I hesitated.

I forced a laugh.

Go on. With a what? And I'll tell you something else just in case you're interested; I haven't been out of this house all week. I haven't moved. I don't think I've even spoken.

I didn't bloody beat him up, I shouted back forcefully.

Exasperated by me, she slumped down on her cushions, her black hair matted and dishevelled. She was trying to control her breathing. Her face was flabby and bloodless. To my relief, she had ignored my invitation for a drink.

What are you doing here, Niall? she asked me then, more quietly, opening her eyes.

I tried to stare back at her as though I thought her question was meaningless.

You don't know, do you?

I kept silent. The closed curtains accounted for the drained atmosphere of the room.

Where have you been? Can't you find anybody to listen to you? You fed up being sorry for yourself? The doldrums losing their special aesthetic quality? Are you feeling like you don't really matter – like that wee man at the bus stop.

I went towards the door.

What do you expect me to say? she wailed in my wake.

I stopped and turned to face her. The air in the room was jaded and acrid like she had been burning incense the night before.

I haven't been out of this house in days.

I nodded, needlessly. Her eyes closed again.

I can't sleep. The last few days I couldn't go outside the door. I had to phone in sick. I . . .

Her helplessness frightened me – I knew I was supposed to sit on the sofa and hold her.

Is it just because of Emmet or . . .?

She shook her head, annoyed with the question. Then: What if it was?

Have you been to the hospital?

As if you cared.

It might be good for you.

Would it now? she laughed. And why might it be good for me? To rub my nose in it? You don't give a damn about anything but yourself, Niall. Face it. That's why you can't bloody write any more.

I stared at her bedridden, spiteful face, wondering how I would react.

And molesting teenage girls at my friend's funeral isn't going to help you out of it. Where the hell have you been since then? You can't just turn up and . . .

She didn't finish what she wanted to say to me. I had sat down on the floor, in a corner beside the window. I think I was crying. She called my name but I couldn't answer. Exhausted beyond words, I found myself praying for an end to my life, which added up to nothing more than pointless bursts of lust and hope. This prayer was made more desperate by the feeling that I had lost the power to even laugh at myself. Horror, love, madness, desire, transgression, all the jubilant songs of excess – everything that could take us beyond ourselves seemed at that moment to be a swindle, a smokescreen, a tamed faked sun to fly towards, to bleed us dry and keep us from seeing that there was nothing beyond our grasp, nothing more, and that all our rage and dreams were prisons. I wanted to die rather than endure any more of this presumptuous wrangling. You're a scaremonger, that's all, a grandiose lunatic who cries wolf every evening amid the rush-hour traffic.

After staring at me for a while, Lorna slowly sank back on the sofa. The afternoon passed without another a word between us. She fell asleep. Later on, I was sitting in the same position with the pieces of her sketch of the forest children spread out before me. Lorna had handed them to me in a plastic bag. I tried to remember if it had been me who had torn up the painting or whether it was Lorna; I didn't want to know.

I went out, saying I was going to the off-licence – I had no intention of coming back. Lorna put all her energy into behaving more cheerfully when I returned. She apologized for her attack on me and her behaviour at the funeral. Her hair was brushed and she had put on a grey linen dress and her woollen poncho. As she tidied the room around me, playing unskilfully at flirtatiousness, I found myself compelled to lower my eyes – I tried to avoid the thought that I was feeling ashamed of her inaccurate coyness.

She was luxuriantly drunk after a few drinks. By whatever means I pressed her for more information, she refused to say very much about what had been troubling her through the week, and why she couldn't sleep or leave the house. She swept all my questions away with an exaggerated and ungainly flick of her hand. Unable to sit still, and drinking heavily, she began to tell me about other periods in her life when she had been tortured by fears and moments of extraordinary pointlessness. She admitted that in these moods she often felt self-destructive but she was incapable of describing in what way or to what degree she wanted to harm herself. The world was hardening around her, she told me, the sky and the air merging with the earth into one smooth hideous crust, and there was no room for her. She also mentioned a man in a red glitter suit who tore strips off the ground like wallpaper. This was as much as I could discover. At the time, I didn't treat her seriously at all.

I'll be OK, she said to me, sucking a piece of lemon between her teeth. It's just a bad patch. It happened before and it just goes away. Lorna Doom, I call myself. The doctor keeps bringing it back to the Bogside – mind I told you about it, when I was standing there one day on the street, when I was about six?

Her throat was speckled with red blotches. She picked a stone from the tip of her tongue.

The man kneeling down behind you? And it was sunny.

She smiled at the fact that I remembered: You know when you have the sun on your face and feel you are drifting out of yourself?

She acted this out, throwing back her head and opening her mouth to the imaginary sun.

And he molested you.

She stumbled backwards as though she had lost her balance. She looked at me oddly, with fear: What . . . are you talking about?

You said some man was feeling you up on the street. He was telling you not to turn round and to stay still.

He had a bloody gun on my shoulder, she shouted at me. Are you stupid?

She careered around the room, muttering curses, stooping for no apparent reason. In this condition, she drank two more gins.

I was the first to speak: I misunderstood maybe, that's all. There's no call for being so angry.

All you think about is sex, she screamed at me with unbridled ferocity.

Maybe you should think some more about it, I said back, muffling my voice.

She heard me but she chose to ignore it. Crying profusely, she slapped her left shoulder: Here . . . right here. I didn't even hear the shot. He used me as a . . . to lean on. This woman coming down the other side of the street wheeling a pram. She just fell against the wall. I didn't hear a sound – like she'd been pushed. Then a red stain. I just stood there, I didn't understand. Sun . . . and silence. Sun and silence like . . . Then one of the neighbours ran over and a whole crowd . . . and my mother took me into the house. . . . And do you know what? None of them ever said a word to me about it. They bought me an ice cream and no one ever asked me if I was OK. It was never mentioned, in the house, or the street, nobody.

So why did they shoot her?

I heard somewhere she was supposed to be going out with a soldier, Lorna said, falling back on the sofa. Who knows?

She tried to laugh.

I knew I should make myself say something. In an attempt to cheer her up, I said: By the way, I was lying in bed the other morning and some of your hair floated down and landed on my face. It's all over my room. Do you ever comb it? It'll still be falling right now as we speak. I've been picking it out of the carpet, big clumps of it, and putting it on the windowsill for the birds. Bunches of it.

You're giving it to the birds? she screeched at me.

I nodded, and shrugged. Her face grimaced into despair. What?

No, she moaned. Tell me you didn't.

They'll use it for their nests just. It's spring.

With her hand over her mouth, she ran into the bathroom. She stayed in there for nearly an hour; I knocked on the door but she wouldn't answer me. It was night by then. There was a crowd of about twenty people at the corner of the street, watchful and taciturn, and some boys running with crates through the dark, when I looked out of the window. Some of the new streetlights were smashed. I drank some more in front of the TV. Losing my patience, I decided to leave, but the crowd had almost doubled in size and I didn't want to risk making my way through them.

While I sat on the floor, I talked to Lorna through the locked bathroom door. I told her about the gathering crowd, about meeting Martina and the macabre children at the bus stop – I made up a story about the purifier, that I had seen him on the street, and chased him for hours through the housing estates but he had got away from me. I swore to her that he had recognized me and grinned in the moment before I set off after him.

Lorna was sitting on the edge of the bath, leaning forward, one hand supporting her forehead, rocking herself and drunkenly eyeing the lifeless swing of her hair above the white tiles. She was thinking back to the nights she shared a bed with Phil and how, to keep herself awake and away from dreams, she used to lie with her hand out on the window ledge. Spiders made webs between her fingers; moths hid from the rain under her palm; snails decorated her with translucent spirals; her nails were black and smelled of moss in the morning. Then there was the night she screamed and thought something had gripped her hand and tried to pull her through the window. Phil woke and she confessed to him. That was the last night he slept in the bed with her.

4

A young man was masturbating in front of the line of police. Some of the crowd were calling for him to stop; he held a petrol bomb in his other hand, which a boy of about ten was

135

trying to set alight. Moving around them were others who carried doors and corrugated metal sheets for protection. I tried to appear sober in the midst of them. Like shadows under the water, the police stood motionless behind the transparent phalanx of shields at the end of the next street. Someone gave me a football scarf to cover my face. Two young girls flitted about in their nightdresses. A three-legged dog barked and pissed itself with excitement.

I had kicked in the door of the bathroom and found Lorna drawing on the mirror with a lipstick. She smiled at me as though she had forgotten the last few hours and then had the idea of putting some make-up on me; I agreed without hesitation, hoping it would comfort her. As she was painting my eyes and lips, I pulled down the straps of her dress and played with her nipples. In a sensual voice, she warned me that I was asking too much of her, that she wasn't able to love anything. I argued with her that the ugliness was all my fault. Her breasts smelled sour and humid. Then she pulled down my trousers and decorated my cock with the lipstick. Neither of us spoke. She tried to resist when I lifted her dress but I pushed her against the sink and went into her from behind – the make-up left stains like blood on her buttocks.

No one blocked my way through the crowd. I was disappointed to see only about ten teenagers at the front-line, leading the disorder. It was after midnight. Everyone else was watching unconcernedly: groups of young men drinking cans of beer and looking around at the girls, a few women chatting, some of the older men in groups with their hands in their pockets as though it was a gesture of devoutness. A boy, stripped to the waist, floated on a mattress in the middle of the street, dangling his hands in the sea of bricks and glass. Picking up whatever was to hand, I ran towards the police, delighting in each thump of the stone against their ice-like shields.

A man with a crowbar leaned into my ear and told me to fuck off back to wherever I came from and wash my face. I withdrew to the fringes and sat down beside an old man, who took one look at me and began to talk about the prostitutes he had known on his travels. Near us, three men of my own age were talking and swigging from a bottle of cider.

Get out of the car, we were telling her. We need your car, missus. Then she goes to us: You can do whatever you want to me but don't touch the car. Please don't touch the car. A rich bitch, big car, perfume, all made up. The wee skirt up round her hips. You should have seen the eyes on her.

So did you take her up on it?

Too right we did. Up a back lane. Four of us. She stood against the wall. No underwear or anything on her.

You're talking crap, Scrum.

I swear to fuck. And listen: about an hour later there she is back again. I swear to Jesus. You can do whatever you want with me but please don't touch the car. She didn't give a damn about the car. This city, I'm telling you boys – it's going downhill fast.

I wasn't sure how to take what he was saying. Moving on to another group, I was ignored when I asked if they had heard about the speaker. A telephone pole was smouldering at the end of the street, a gargantuan dreamlike turd. Wedged above us, the night sky seemed soiled and smashed like stained glass in a derelict chapel. I drifted back into the main crowd and threw a blackened metal bolt at a police Land-Rover. There was a sickened cheer then as the teenager finally managed to make himself come in the forlorn alluvium of no-man's-land. At the limit of disgust, one of the cops threw aside his shield and made a run for the boy, but not before some of the other rioters got him out of the way. The boy was put into the hands of two men who took him up a back lane; we heard him screaming a few minutes later.

The boy's beating coincided with the police breaking their ranks and charging towards us, some of them without shields, the Land-Rovers spreading out behind them. Land-Rovers appeared out of the dark wherever I looked. A beam from a helicopter lit up the street. I ran blindly, down an alley, then another, across a flooded square, tensing myself at every corner and turn for the sudden detonation of headlights in my face and the salvo of shouts I would have to obey. The fear seemed to empty me like a final confession of – I choked on my own self-pity. All around me the dogs were barking crazily. Every door was shut, the windows dark. On some street, I lay down behind a car but failed to convince myself that I was safe . . . After that a dog ran alongside me, snapping playfully at my feet in spite of my curses, as though I was nothing more than a moving shadow. My greatest desire was to see someone on the street, a woman smoking a cigarette at the window, a drunk, any lunatic of the night – all I wanted was to speak, to slow myself down because I couldn't conceive of being able to bring this petrified scarper to a halt by myself.

On the Lone Moor Road, the noise of a Land-Rover sent me towards a wall, which I couldn't find a grip on . . . I ran across the road again, and pulled myself up on the bars of a gate. Hitting the ground on the other side, I damaged my ankle and had to roll into some bushes as a paint-splattered Jeep went slowly along the road. I lay still, concentrating my mind on the pain, praying for it not to fade and leave me alone (I had the mad idea that the pain and the ruined make-up on my face was all that was between me and some kind of invisibility; my glamorized cock was stiff in my trousers). It was only when I willed myself back on my feet to increase the pain that I saw I had climbed the gate into the cemetery. Holding my breath, I hopped on my bad ankle and fell flat on my face again.

I couldn't get back over the gate. With nowhere else to go, I started up the slope between the split-open crypts and debauched supplicating angels, dragging my foot. Without acknowledging it to myself, I must have known where I was going. The helicopters, two wands of light now, seemed to be scything out of the dark any memory of the sun and revolt. Slowly, the fear faded, leaving me disappointed, as though I had been cheated by something. I pushed my foot down hard with each step up the slope between the trees, laughing at the pain. There was a memorial wreath hanging on a broken Celtic cross; I flung the thing out across the graves as a challenge.

Martina had once described the location of my father's grave. I thought I hadn't been paying much attention but I was able to find his plot without too much trouble. They had put up a plain black slab; without light, I tried to decipher the inscription in the marble with my fingertips. There were flowers in a metal pot; a low railing around the rectangle of pale gravel; at the foot of the grave, a white stone to kneel on. Without a second thought, I lay down on top of the grave, laughing to myself when I had to rest my ankles on the rail so that I could fit.

Think about him – your wank-stain of a father, I demanded of myself. My mind couldn't manage the simplest thing. The darkness sucked me out of myself completely. The city lay buried in a shallow grave of lights and tiny hopes. What did you teach me? I cried out. That life of yours, what did you use it for? Mute and obedient to the end in your fraying suits, your handkerchief under your knees at mass, the crime novels in the kitchen at night. Did you ever know a sigh of pleasure? Did you ever lose all hope for yourself on my mother's breasts? What did you use your life for? What should I do with the memory of your life? Your pride and baldy uprightness was a mask of fear. That vitriolic night of whiskey with your brother – I was listening on the stairs as you cursed everything in your life, your wife and children and the struggle for freedom you taught me to think was beneath me. And in the morning you went to mass and came back to wash the spuds. You crossed yourself in shame if the sun came out. Coward . . . coward – servitude . . . Do you hear me now in your great realm of failure? I hope the rats laughed their heads off at you as they rinsed their mouths in your wasted eyes and sucked the last moan from the end of your fasting tongue.

I must have fallen asleep up there. When I opened my eyes, it was light, birds were jumping and singing all around me, and a voluptuous blue sky spread itself like a dreaming woman above me. I thought I was back in Italy and for an instant I was filled with joy. I tried to get up but my ankle made me shout with pain and almost immediately I fell back on the ground, and remembered where I was. In the fresh wind, the cords rattled and chimed on the Volunteers' flag-poles. The dew clung to the cemetery hill, sparkling in the paths of the wind.

As I lay there, I saw a metal sign, in black and white, stuck in the tidy grass at the end of the line of graves which said: DOGS MUST BE KEPT ON A LEASH. At first, I thought this was sensible, since they might get in the way at a funeral or cause embarrassment. Then, once I had finally managed to get on my feet, I looked down at my father's grave and saw to my horror that the gravel was scattered and there were obvious traces of digging . . . I gaped at the dirt on my hands, under my fingernails, on my clothes. Even the skin on my face felt like it was heavy with dirt. There was grit under my tongue, in my gums – falling to my knees, I puked.

PART SEVEN

In the days following the incident in the cemetery, I didn't leave my bed. A fever hunted me in and out of consciousness. I was drawn back into the same repulsive dream time after time: digging with the last of my strength at my father's grave, the children gathered in a vast crowd all around me, naked, seized by diabolical fits, holding burning torches, their faces painted white; I knew that if I didn't obey them they would tear me to pieces.

I lay for more than a day alone in that room, knowing that I wasn't strong enough to look after myself. I couldn't even find the energy to worry about what would happen to me. One day, around dusk, I woke up, soaked in sweat, startled by a joy that was about to tear my heart open: I thought I was dying then. Why did I not feel afraid?

Danny says I let him into the flat but I have no memory of it. I see him feeding me soup he had asked his mother to make; I see him in front of my window in bright sunshine, combing his hair, and as he steps aside, a smoke-ring of black and blood-red smoke suspended above the roofs; snoring in his sleeping bag alongside my bed, empty tins of beer around his head like a talisman; chasing a fly around the room with a rolled-up paper; with the doctor in the kitchen, smiling as though he is waiting for the end of a joke, and then at the last moment, he bows his head and bites his tongue as he used to do at school when he was caught talking.

Danny, you have to do me a favour, I said to him, waking out of another dream. He was sitting in the chair with a book. You have to, Danny. There's something I didn't tell you the other night – when was it? There was a riot and I ended up in the cemetery and –

You told me.

No, I didn't, Danny. I couldn't have.

You did. The other night. You've been talking about it in your sleep anyway. Some gang of wains are after you. You're dreaming just.

He held up the book to look at a photograph in better light.

I was digging at my Da's grave, Danny. Do you hear me?

And I was a great singer in this band and we were touring the world, and the women were falling at my feet.

You have to go and look at my Da's grave for me, I begged him, sitting up in the bed, squinting. The room was full of light, too much fervid white light; I couldn't see anything clearly.

It won't have moved.

You have to, Danny. I'm sick. It's driving me mad. I can't trust anybody else.

He laughed sceptically to himself: Look for what, anyway?

Just look at it and tell me what you see. I swear, Danny, I need you to. Just look at it and come back and tell me.

Right now?

I swear, Danny; it's not a joke.

The cemetery? Did you forget something or what? Like your bloody brain? I have to go to work in a while, you know.

He closed the book and hit himself on the head with it. Then he waved a bare arm towards the window and said: And look at the weather – probably the only bit of sun we'll get this century and you're sending me up to the cemetery.

Just check it's . . . the way it should be.

He threw the book on the bed and stood up. He was wearing shorts. The book was some history of socialism in Ireland. The light kept flowering in harsh bursts around the room. On the floor was a cracked bowl with two spoons in it – the thought of Danny's mother scraping wrinkled hairy vegetables into a pot in her dark scullery made me wonder if I wasn't still dreaming.

Danny raised his hands over his head and stretched himself, yawning: So are you back in the land of the living? I'm only going to do this because you're sick, right?

144

There was a knock at the door then, which made me panic and flounder about in the bed.

Don't let him in, I warned Danny in a whisper. I'm not here.

Who? he laughed.

Just don't. Our Michael.

It's Lorna.

Sneering, he nodded when I checked his face to see if he was serious.

I asked her to stay away, he said darkly.

Pretending to be asleep, I listened to them talking together for a few minutes at the door. Danny called out that he was away and I listened to the luckless medley of Lorna's jewellery as she came into the room. After a few minutes, she said my name. I lay still, becoming aware of her bitter perfume. The squall of creaks when she sat down in the chair was torture to listen to.

I know you can hear me, she said. Are you OK?

She talked for a long time – a subdued, disordered, tearless monologue, broken by long silences during which I could hear her breathing, almost panting, and the noise of the chair. She told me as much as her loyalty would allow about Phil, and their years in Belfast, and how she was so depressed she did not really notice that he had left her and gone to London. She talked about her father; for weeks after the shooting incident he used to lift her above his head and shake her triumphantly and tell her how proud he was. Standing by the window, she described the events and thoughts that had led her towards socialism. After her longest silence, and saying my name a few times, she led me through some of her dreams – and the feeling of fraught precipitant emptiness that took over her.

. . . That's how I feel . . . like one of those old photos in the hotel Danny is always going on about, that might be fakes. I'm a bad montage, curling at the edges. But I was talking about us, wasn't I? You're right. I know you're bored with me . . . and I can't give you what you want. I'm always losing

145

heart, I know that. We've just met . . . I keep forgetting that – we both do, I think. And you're right about stifling everything with rules and commitment; I lose perspective on too many things, so suddenly . . . I forget everything I believe. Life's too short . . . and our actions outlive us – you would say our desires outlive us. So I say we try to start again . . . and see what happens. And you just have to ignore me when I lose my head and think the world is going to end . . . and I'm sorry for painting your face; no wonder you got . . . I can't believe you even let me . . .

One day, weeks before, I had seen her on a bus, as I was walking around the city centre (this is one of the thoughts I let my mind dwell on as a way of expurgating her sentimental attempt to rationalize our relationship). Looking straight ahead, she sat stiffly by the bus window, which someone had sprayed their name over. Beside her there was a teenage girl with a bunch of yellow roses, who at that very moment offered Lorna the flowers to smell. From where I stood on the street, I saw Lorna shake her head to decline and then turn slowly towards the window where she stared keenly out through the graffiti at the street and the rain and an army checkpoint.

I kept up the pretence of sleep until Danny returned from the cemetery. I tried to catch his eye but he always managed to be doing something else, tidying my room, or trying to make Lorna laugh with stories about the hotel. Eventually, I asked him directly how things were and he said casually, while showing Lorna a page in his book, that they were no better or worse than expected. I wanted to shout at him; he was hiding from me.

Both of them left together.

2

The window was wide open. It must have been near midday because the Spaniards were gathered in the flat below. Lorna and Danny were sitting on the floor; I listened to their talk as though they were strangers. Lorna rested against the end of the bed, her hair pinned up. Danny had a question for her each time she finished speaking; I couldn't detect any trace of sarcasm in his voice. Lorna went through the reasons behind some sit-in she was obviously devoting much of her time to. The speaker's name came up, so I took it that he must have recovered and left the hospital.

Lorna laughed – a laugh I hadn't heard before, sorrowful but tender and full of shyness. The air was light and sweet that day. They had been talking for a long time, I seemed to understand. Danny lowered his voice and said that he had been thinking about me, and about whether I was right to come back; he used to believe that people never grew out of where they came from but now he wasn't so sure. Lorna took a minute before she admitted that she often had the same thoughts but she always reminded herself that I tried too hard not to fit in. Danny then told her a story about us as teenagers, about a drunken night when the two of us were attacked outside a disco; I had started to laugh uncontrollably as they kicked at me, which resulted in the two of us getting a more severe beating than was normal. This was almost our last night out together before I left. He was glad to be getting out of here, he said to Lorna; they could have taken an iron bar to him and he wouldn't have stopped laughing. He had it easier than anybody I know but he hated the place.

Later that day, I told Lorna that I didn't remember Danny's story. It had been a long, gentle, radiant dusk. She had made some food and lit candles around the room.

Whatever, you look better, she said. There's some colour back in your face. You're missing all the good weather.

You're not listening to me, I accused her. I listened to you about the shooting. I didn't ignore you as though you were making it up, did I? And you might have been, for all I know.

I was listening, she said, taking my hand.

Maybe he's lying.

Come off it. Why would he do that? she said, attempting to soothe me.

You're trying to recruit him, aren't you? You know he's mad about you.

No, he's not, she said gently. He wants direction. He's thinking about things.

You're patronizing him. You sit there flirting with him and then you look down your nose at him. I bet you don't patronize Mr Speaker – Martin or whatever you call him? Is he out of hospital then?

Without a word, she laid her head on my chest, trying to calm me. I've been thinking about going away for a while, she said. I know a wee house on the Sligo coast. I was going to ask if you wanted to come. It would do the both us the world of good. There's nothing important here, is there? You could do some writing.

I don't want to do any bloody writing, I said, and meant it.

She waited again: Or do you think I'm just running away?

Run, I told her.

I went to see the doctor again and you know what he said? It's only natural for a woman of my age. Can you believe it? He meant because I was on my own. The look on his face when he heard I wasn't married . . . I'm only thirty-two, not fifty.

Her weight on my chest, and her scented hair covering my mouth made it difficult to breathe. I pushed her off me; her cleavage hung down before, moist with sweat. For a long time, she seemed to forget herself and stared at me – with an avid certainty in her eyes that made me uncomfortable. She laughed at me suddenly, then looked thoughtful.

Blow out those candles; I'm not dead yet, I said.

The smoke carried the smell of almonds around the room. Putting the pillows behind my head, I told her that I wanted to watch her masturbate. She tried not be surprised at my directness, and refused wordlessly. She sat down in the chair by the window.

Are you sure? she said, smiling.

Keep your clothes on.

She was wearing tights under her crumpled silk skirt. She closed her eyes as her hands reached her broad inner thighs. Pulling the waist of the tights away, her other hand went down between her legs.

I'm watching you, I said.

Her head fell forward on her chest. As the sun poured down on her, she rubbed and dug at herself until there was not the slightest hint of eroticism left, and then on into the realms of repulsion. She failed to come. Finally, sweating, she flung herself on the bed, face down. It grew dark. With her face buried in the pillow, her hand searched for a way under the blankets. Then, to my surprise, she knelt up and climbed on top of me. She pulled the metal clasp out of her hair, and unbuttoned her blouse.

I want to, she said, with stark gravity.

I let her do all the work. Giving myself over to a fantasy about the brimming, imperious trance of the girl on the night-train through France, I managed to make myself come. Lorna dropped heavily on the bed beside me, and asked if I would hold her; every part of her was slimy with sweat and disappointment.

3

The next morning I felt much better and Lorna did not have to try very hard to persuade me to leave the bedsit for a walk in the park. She went home quickly and returned with a camera. Our cheerfulness as we walked the short distance to the park was apparent to people passing on the street, who all nodded and would have stopped to talk to us if I had given them a chance. The sun continued to reign in the Derry sky, a suicide's scream over the dour diatribe of the streets – Lorna, of course, thought it was all raw and charming.

She made me laugh that day, more than any other. As we passed her uncle's house, she told me how he had run off on his family to America, where he found his way into cowboy films as the witless drunk who was continually thrown through the doors of the saloon into a puddle in the street. He made a fortune, married again, and bought himself a big ranch. She was full of stories that day, one for every street we came to.

Your turn now. You're the writer. She laughed at my consternation.

The park was on a slope like the cemetery. The army surveillance tower, overloaded with red lights, radar discs and camouflaged netting, was more conspicuous than I remembered it. Lorna told me about a pressure group who wanted the tower dismantled. At a lazy pace, we were following the paths that cut across the grass and the freshly planted flowerbeds. A man, bared to the waist, was digging around some bushes, and his two dogs watched him from the shade.

I let her take some photos of me. One, which I still have, is of me looking hunched and finished in front of a tree; some European artist had been allowed to cut holes in the trunks and insert pieces of mirrored glass in an effort at a symbol of reflection and reconciliation, a plaque informed us.

We sat down on the grass, Lorna in the shadow cast by the ruin of the old asylum building, which we both thought had all the characteristics of a hallucination in the soft unmoving sunlight. The back of the building had collapsed, pulling down most of the roof, except for a few long beams which someone called Pontious had managed to decorate with his name and a variety of glue-inspired riddles at impossible angles. Between the mounds of fallen stones, the small barred windows of the cells were visible just above the ground. It had been a library in later days as well, Lorna reminded me.

But what about the cells? The library kept the bars in the windows . . . and no glass. The cells are down there intact. We used to drink in them. Me and Danny, and other people as well. There was an old prostitute lay down there; she was about fifty, an alco, ugly. You'd pay her with some fags for her to pull you off. She was useless. She used to sing her head off some nights down there in the cells, and take off her clothes and roll in the dirt. Rats running around . . . complete darkness. And then she just vanished. At the time we all thought she had been killed, to get rid of her. For corrupting the minds of the youngsters . . . out of their brains on glue and drink.

Lorna wouldn't believe me; she was sure I was making it up. I told her about another night, with only Danny and myself. It wasn't long before I was leaving for university, one of those weekends when we drank in the building through the night, cheap cider mostly, without ever asking ourselves why we weren't at the pub or the disco like everybody else, stumbling around on the masonry, the rain beating down in the locked-up park.

This particular night, driven by boredom or the cold, we began to throw stones at each other. It was a game to start off with, but it quickly developed into a savage hunt for each other among the ruins.

We were going to kill each other, I said to Lorna. I'm not joking. I was terrified. If he had cornered me he would have stoned me to death. And me, him . . . Listening for each other's footsteps, not daring to breathe . . . hiding in the pitch dark down there. We were hunting each other. It lasted all night. I still remember seeing the dawn through the bars in the cell window . . . exhausted. The park was full to above the trees with a white mist. Everything was wet. I was waiting for Danny to come through the door and break my skull.

Danny? It's not in him. Lorna laughed, shielding her eyes from the sun. Did he get you then?

I started calling his name, cursing him, so he could find me and we would get it over with . . . and I waited. Another hour or so. It was a Sunday and the bells went for first mass. But he didn't show. In the end, I went out into the mist, filthy with dirt, tired out. I waited down there beside that old sycamore – I pointed it out for Lorna – and then I saw him come out. He didn't see me.

151

So what happened?

He climbed up a tree.

Like hell he did. Lorna showed her disbelief by rummaging in her bag.

He did. Disappeared up into the mist. And after a while I climbed up too . . . and we went to sleep up in the tree for a couple of hours. You should have seen the faces of the mass-goers when we jumped down amongst them, covered in dirt out a tree.

Lorna was pointing her camera at me. There, I got you this time, she said, pleased with herself. The building in the background too . . . and smiling to yourself as well.

It was just boredom, I said, scowling then, and trying to talk away my irritation with her and her camera. Boredom is my main impression of growing up in this place.

Boredom is an effect of capitalist hyperconsumption, she said complacently, and lay back on the grass, her arm across her eyes. She sighed: You know, I don't think I like parks. They're too permanent and fixed. Like stuffed landscapes. Still lifes.

Not socialist enough for you? Your crowd builds parks and monuments as well. And a lot bigger.

You may as well be in a museum . . . or a cemetery, she said, and she was squinting at the sky, with what I thought was the curl of a smile on her lips. She was overdressed for the sun, all in black; she hated the sun. A cold unease spread through me.

Has Danny said anything to you?

About what?

I was still confused about how much Danny knew about what had happened in the cemetery, or whether or not he believed it was only a dream on my part. I hadn't said a word to Lorna about any of it; the reasons for my silence were outlandish in themselves. The notion occurred to me, as I stared at Lorna lifeless on the grass, that Danny had told her everything on his return from the cemetery, about my dream, or worse; about what he had seen up there.

Has Danny said anything to you? I heard myself asking her again, my voice trembling.

The two of them in my room, whispering in the dark while I lay in my bed, foaming with dread – no, it wasn't that; what appalled me about her smile was that she was assuming some responsibility for the dream – that she thought it belonged to her, and that I was only a victim. Worse than pity, she thought my state of mind was all her own her doing.

As soon as the idea entered my head, I believed it. The flicker of a smile on her lips was transfigured into a blatant grin of evil. She thinks it's her fault and she's not even sorry, I said to myself, breathless and terrified; she thinks it's just what she deserves . . . or we deserve. My fingers dug into the hard ground. Some children had come into the park with a ball. A woman on a bench stretched her legs. The dogs chased each other around in the fountain.

Lorna . . . I said. It's impossible to describe the mixture of hope and trepidation in my voice as I waited to see her face. Lorna, I'm feeling really ill again. Do you hear me? I need you to look at me.

She sat up, blinking, some grass in her hair.

What? she said and I heard the alarm in her voice. Was I asleep?

She reached out her hand, her painted nails, and with profound relief, I grabbed it – I held on to her hand as though it was my own heart she had offered me.

4

It was two days later that I knocked on my brother's door with the conviction that the time had come at last for us to face each other. I hurried through the rain to his house as if he was waiting impatiently on me to arrive, Martina and Louise out of the way for the night, and him with his elbows on the draining board, looking out the kitchen window at the empty coal shed. I was convinced he was calling me, or at least thinking about me; the idea presented itself to me while I was in the process of tearing up something I had written, and it wouldn't be pushed aside.

I was drenched by the time I arrived outside his door. A light went on in the hall. But it was an old woman's face that looked out through a gap in the door. Eventually, I realized it was my Auntie Charlotte. She didn't recognize me; she thought I knew Michael from work. They've gone over the border to some dance, she whispered to me, almost slyly. She didn't invite me in.

The rain failed to drive me back home – the rain gushed along the gutters in the old empty streets, made a dose of puddles at every corner and fell through the dreamy light of the new culs-de-sac of red brick, but the city was a corpse, beyond solace, that nothing could ever clean or enliven. I jeered at myself for ever thinking I was any different. My heart, my desire for a life that was a sumptuous, swooning transcendence, was drowned and sank out of sight.

Cheer up, a bouncer under the awning of a new pub called out to me. It's only a bit of water.

Fuck off back to jail, I told him and ran.

I went through the doors of the cathedral and sat down near a radiator and a bank of candles – my sole motive for entering was to mock myself. Rain dripped from me onto the bench, the paved floor and the padded kneeling rail. Two old women knelt side by side in front of the altar, their scarves drying on the back of the bench. I knelt also, with a vague poisonous desire to offer up my submission for the sake of somebody, Michael or anyone. As I used to do as a child, I gnawed at the wood of the seat in front of me. My mind began to wander, searching for a memory, or a prayer. The whispering of the two old women reached me, then their laughter . . . I watched them hurry out, arm in arm, biting their lips, and the candles swayed around me as the door swung shut behind them.

In silence, tasting the wood and varnish in my mouth, I began to pray, for Martina and Louise, then for fear of myself, and then for all people, young and old, men and women, the wild and the tamed, the frivolous or the despondent, military or civilian, that we might all abandon our homes, our cars and schools, our offices and barracks, our churches, our factories and suburbs, and turn our backs for good on all work, all striving, all obligations, all right and wrong and collect in the streets and refuse, screaming out our refusal, to ever lift a finger again.

Be a god, I prayed, be a true god, even as I heard a door creak open on the other side of the chapel. A dark-haired woman walked under a lamp and knelt down, resting her forehead on her joined hands. I knew it was her immediately, her walk, the slow procedure of lowering herself to her knees – Lorna, saying her penance after confession.

I began to shake with the pressure of trying to control my violence. I wanted to drag her by the hair from the seat, trail her up to the altar and punish her – but a fittingly grotesque punishment was beyond my imagination. What was she confessing? How dare she confess? Is she praying for herself, or somebody else – for me? These questions shook my entire body.

Earlier that same day, she had woken up in my bed, around dusk. The clouds were moving in after the open days of sun; smoke lurked nervously around the chimneys and flies circled in the room. She had slept for an hour after her stint at the sit-in; while she slept, I went on with the story I had begun writing.

I just feel lifeless, she said. Ugly and sterile. Emmet asked me to do some leafleting and I had to tell him no. I feel detached from everything.

After a few minutes she asked what I was doing.

Writing.

Who to?

A story.

She sat up in the bed: Really? You're writing? She stumbled across the room, when she was sure I wasn't looking, and put her arms around me.

155

I'm so pleased, Niall. I really am. It's so good.

I let her kiss my face.

I'll get out of your hair, she said, lifting her coat and going straight for the door – she was the type of woman who can get out of bed and go straight out the door without checking her look in the mirror.

It's going to pour.

I'll be all right. You carry on, she said, smiling motherly. So get on with it, she scolded me for staring.

I tore up everything I had written after she went. Her excitement on my behalf revolted me.

She finished her penance, got to her feet, and then knelt again to pray quickly for something, blessing herself. I thought of accosting her; following her for a street or two and then listening to her lie about where she had been. In the end, I stood in the cathedral porch behind a pillar, and watched her wander unconsoled off into the unsparing rain. She was in no hurry. I threw a candle after her that I had picked up inside, then another, and another, making sure not to be seen. The noise of her army boots running away in terror across the wet gravel did little to soothe me.

5

I was over for a look at the sit-in, Danny said, without a trace of discomposure. There's a fair crew of people down there. Twenty-four hours a day.

The wind exploded along the street outside the café; leaves and rubbish and sand hit the windows – the air was full of sand from under the clawed-up paving stones, Danny informed me. He had caught some sun on his face and his eyes were cold and lively.

The old people don't want to move, that's the problem. They've been there all their lives, paying rent all their lives – the council just decide to sell it to developers one morning and expect them to just pack up without a word. The council are offering them places in parts of the town they don't even know exist. They're too scared to go anywhere . . . Lorna was there, Danny added, as if to back up his argument.

The waitress was drowsily observing Danny's enthusiasm in the quiet café.

I couldn't keep the sarcasm out of my voice: So are you thinking of getting involved then?

He shrugged: Thinking about it, that's all. I've been thinking about a lot of things. The socialist crowd, if you ask me, are the only people who make any sense. Nobody else said a word about the old people until the socialists starting making an issue of it. I've been talking to Lorna a bit about it, you know?

We looked each other in the eye for a few seconds, fruitlessly.

I've been thinking about a lot of things, Danny said again.

Let me know what you find out.

Danny leaned towards me: There's going to be changes, don't you think? You can feel it. More talks, decisions – I don't know, but it won't go on the way it did, that's all. It can't now. Different questions are being asked nowadays, over the whole country, don't you think?

I wouldn't know, Danny, I said, and waited to see what honesty would waken inside me. A wind that had never heard tell of the mountains or the sea attacked the windows with a fury that made me uneasy and despondent.

Unconvincingly, Danny jabbed at the table with his finger: It's the middle classes on both sides keeping this all going. The workers in the Protestant estates are as badly off as our lot and they're starting to realize that. You know, there's some Protestant protesters up at the sit-in. That's what all the suits are shit-scared of, you see. Don't you think?

Did Lorna tell you that?

Does it matter who told me if it's right? Danny's face darkened. Nobody else has ever taken the time to say anything to me. I don't want to end up like –

Like what?

I don't know. He shrugged a few times. The last few weeks – I don't want to spend my whole life thinking there's no point in anything, that's all. You know, just going through the motions, then dropping dead. Like most people when you think about it. Just leaving things to everybody else . . . if we all – I don't know.

He folded his thin arms on the table and pressed his lips together. The waitress raised one of her overplucked eyebrows at me but it wasn't clear what she meant; I smiled at her but she remained impassive.

Danny scratched his head and tried again: You see, it's about trying to get over that feeling . . . that it makes no difference what you think anyway, that you've no right to an opinion. What do you think of what I'm saying?

He expected me to answer him; his earnestness could seem farcical at times. As usual, I began to speak without any idea of what I hoped to say.

What I think, Danny, is that the whole thing is a mess. Every bit of it, every street, every institution, every glazed red brick of it, every thought. It's all wrong, deeply wrong, every squandered moment of it . . . including you and me sitting here talking about it.

Is that what you think? Danny turned up his nose at me.

It might be, I said. And what's worse is we're all being wrong deliberately – deliberately.

Sitting here, talking, right now?

Every thought and feeling. And the wind on that street, and that wee boy over there dipping his finger in the sugar, and the waitress there, all fastidious sloth – the whole shebang, deliberately wrong, I told him, growing excited by these ideas as they came to me. Why though? That's the problem. Why are we all lying to ourselves? What are we hiding from?

Whatever it actually means, Lorna called you a bored aesthete, he surprised me by saying.

He was genuinely worried about what he would make of this conversation later on.

158

She's the one who's bored, I said, losing my temper instantly. She'd die before she'd admit it though. Did she ever ask you about her happy gas?

Danny didn't know what I was talking about. I had nothing better to do, so I took a walk with him through the town to see what was happening at the sit-in, with the callous intention of putting Lorna's question to him. We stopped at the river, high and brown and rapid that day, and watched a patrol boat turning in circles at the legs of the bridge that both our fathers had helped to build. We talked about the summer a whale had been trapped in the Foyle, and the crowds that came to see it. Gulls crowded on every ledge, with the pigeons and crows. Danny spoke to a man ripping carpet out of a flooded shop about the damage around the town. Going down the hill into the Bogside, a girl with streaming blonde hair and impressive legs gave us both a bad look as she went by. I took hold of Danny's arm.

What's going on? That was Noreen.

He shrugged and hung his head: We split up.

She won't even speak to you, I said as though I was pointing it out to him.

Danny nodded; he wouldn't meet my eye.

Did she finish with you?

What do you think? He tried to laugh at me for asking the question.

I felt guilty that he hadn't been able to tell me about it but also amused by his secrecy. We didn't bother with the sit-in; I made him come with me for a pint in The Lesson. No one else was drinking that day. The barman was dozing. There were puddles of water in the shiny black ashtrays. A girl came through the door while I was waiting on the pints and left a tray of sandwiches on the bar; I remembered her from school: Eileen – I took off her school blouse inside a concrete pipe on a building site. As she chatted to the barman, she noticed that I was staring at her, that I couldn't take my eyes off her. She was extremely pretty and well dressed. She drew the barman's attention to me as though she was asking who I was;

he glanced at me and then raised his eyes to the ceiling as though there was no point in talking about it.

You look old enough to be her Da anyway, Danny said when I pointed out to him what had happened. I was sure I had never given this particular barman call to have a bad opinion of me.

After only three pints, I knew that I was completely drunk. Danny wasn't listening to me any more. We had both become claustrophobic and galled; Danny was better at controlling himself. I accused him of being weak.

You're not even angry with her. You're too scared to let yourself be angry, I said, hitting him with my elbow.

Glaring at me out of the corner of his eye, he chose not to speak.

Go on. Do you want to hit me?

He blew air heavily out of his nose and mouthed something. What? Say it.

The fucken state of you, he hissed with a contorted face. You just twist everything. No wonder Lorna's on her own.

I had to laugh at that: Listen to Casanova here, dumped again by some wee Derry money-grabber.

Danny's hand left his glass and slowly folded into a fist in front of my face; his hand was hairless, pale and clean. I put on a derisory grin. Although I knew he might hit me, I wasn't thinking of shielding myself. With an inimical tightening of his eyes, he began to carefully lower his fist and brought it down without a sound between our glasses on the table.

You know fuck all about Noreen and fuck all about Lorna, he spat the words out, fingering the black Braille of the cigarette burns in the table . . . I spent a night round there at Lorna's. She asked me to. She needed somebody to talk to. She was desperate not to be on her own . . . And where the fuck were you? Dublin or somewhere? That girl's scared . . . out of her wits.

I had to keep talking to fight off the dizziness. Did you tell Noreen? Is that why she dumped you? You'll never get yourself a decent job now if you hang about them socialist types, you know. You'll never make a good husband, you know, if you're always thinking about how everybody else is doing. You have to be selfish to be kind, you know. You can't be worrying –

I'm no bloody pervert anyway, Danny muttered into his glass before he filled his mouth with stout. He put the emptied glass down and sat back against the wall. My mind flooded itself; I couldn't see. At least a minute or two passed before any words would come to me. Danny was looking towards the door where an old man had appeared with a suitcase. Suddenly I was choking with rage, and my voice had become hoarse.

You wouldn't even know what a pervert is, Danny. Is that what Lorna called me then? A pervert? It's her who's the pervert. What'd she say? I ask too much of her? She can't do the things I want, is that it? It's not sex for her; it's doom and misery. She's the one who adores all the gloom and the suffering. She can't get enough of it, Danny. Did she tell you that? Did she tell you she thinks she's having premonitions she's going to die?

The old man and the barman were looking over at us – as though they had a good right to. Danny inhaled but didn't let it out. I pushed him again with my elbow.

It's my fucken word, he finally burst. You ran off to Dublin with that American one and then you just show up again – it was my fucken word. Pervert. Lorna didn't say it.

The tears in his eyes were not even for himself.

There's worse than that, Danny. There's a lot worse. What about digging up my own Da's grave?

Danny made a grimace of disgust: You fucken knew your Michael would be up there, didn't you? he turned towards me, harrowing and swollen-eyed. I had to stand there and lie to him. He thought it was some animal that did it. And it fucken was – fucken you. Do you have a clue what it took out of me to lie to him? For you who . . .

He couldn't find the words.

I laughed in his face. You should have finished me off that night of the stoning in the old asylum, Danny.

I don't know what the fuck she sees in you.

Did she not tell you about the dreams? The wee man in the red glitter suit. Her poor dreams have broken their moorings, Danny, and they're floating around the place . . . You'd better be careful or you'll end up in one of them. Everything's after her. There's somebody whispering the word cholesterol over and over again when she closes her eyes. Did she tell you that? The wee man in his red suit and the path of perfect white pebbles up to the house. The abandoned town. Couldn't you get them out of your head when you were lying between Noreen's perfect legs? Is that why she dumped you?

With his elbows on the table, Danny gripped the glass with both hands. I was waiting on it to shatter. Suddenly he stood up.

I don't know what the fuck you ever came back here for, he said, and he was looking all over the bar as though he didn't know where he was. You're fucken sick, do you know that?

You just going to walk out now? You're a fucken coward . . . like in the asylum.

He swung his fist at me, blindly – he missed by a long way and fell across the table. I didn't move while he stood up again; he was drunker than I thought. He tried to say something more but the words wouldn't come out of him . . . He spat on the floor. Unsteadily he walked into the middle of the bar and stopped, his back to me. When I looked again he had turned round, struggling with his eyes as he said: And I finished with her. Then he shouted it at me: I fucken finished with her. Right?

I carried on drinking; my destructive self-pity knew no bounds. In the same bar later that night, I cornered some soft-eyed girl, seething with the compulsion to tell her about digging up my father with my bare hands – it was insanely decisive that she understood me. Two men followed me out, and then for a street or two. They called me by my name. I didn't go down under the punches and kicks for they might have hit me with something else, but they made sure I would remember them in the morning.

PART EIGHT

1

The sky darkened finally as I reached the cottage again. I had been walking for hours through a sunk, wounded light, past fields squatted by gangs of ancient stones, abandoned farmhouses, secret black waterways, and the hills that seemed to have turned their backs on their world. I met no one on the roads. The big, curdling evening sun cloyed on me as much as the regret that I had been enticed away from the city by Lorna's dreams of isolation and peace. At the very point when, almost gladly, I had given up finding my way back, a woman in a headscarf gave me a lift as far as the shores of a lough. Children's voices reached me from a wooded island out in the shining, trampled water.

I knocked for too long a time on the small, buckled door. Going round the back of the cottage, I decided to smash a hole in the kitchen window and searched for a stone. The glass made hardly any noise. I waited anyway before opening the latch and climbing in. The house was already swamped with darkness. In the living room, the damp, clouded air left a foul taste of soil at the back of my throat.

I remember I withdrew my hand from the light switch, preferring to remain in the dark. The bare angry shape of things in the room struck me with awe – the darkness tempted each thing with its lethal comfort but nothing gave way: a dented bucket; a stack of peat; a mildewed cushion; a wagon wheel hung on a chain from the ceiling; empty wine bottles on the long table and, on the stone floor, a cap that I had thrown off in despair the night before – my heart began to grieve for the agonized pulse of these things. Each of them had the tragic robbed quality of a newborn child, the half-open door where she had planted the hatchet, my bag dumped in the armchair in the corner – a grim, suckling, bloodless hunger. Through the window, the stars appeared bright and distant and humourless at this blind spawning.

You nearly killed me.

That would be just what you want.

Because I offended you? I'd want a much better reason.

We all want things we can't have.

You don't believe that for a second.

I don't force myself to believe what I say.

Well then, why do you force it on me?

Lorna was right. Seated against the wall, I hadn't seen her when I came in.

We were driving along; this is what I remember. Just let me talk through it. Because I don't understand. Is that OK? she asked with overdone sarcasm, a touch of an English accent in her voice.

Grunting, I stood with my back to her.

We were driving along . . . the road was empty. We went over the brow of a hill. Nothing in front of us or behind. It's a beautiful evening, the sun is going down. Sublime . . . and calm. Gentleness everywhere. Emptiness. Silence . . . dying colours – and then you say: We are dead.

We could be dead; that's what I said, I corrected her. We could have hit a wall and died without knowing it. Or crashed suddenly and we hadn't realized it yet. I was joking. There was a strange atmosphere . . .

Each of us spoke in a lugubrious voice in that dark, writhing room.

I'm sorry, I told her.

No, hold on. Then you said: Imagine we're dead and it's all the same. The afterlife. Everything was exactly the same – the same fields and roads and walls and sky and cities and laws. The same languages after the grave. No differences. That's right, isn't it?

I agreed.

Imagine that everything will be exactly the same as it is now after we die. OK. And then what happens? I say something. What do I say?

166

I was silent and she asked me again. Turning round, I repeated her words to her horribly featureless shadow in the chair: That would be OK.

That wouldn't be so bad – those were my words, she said hastily. That wouldn't be so bad, that's what I said. And what happens next? You go off your head and grab the wheel and spin us off the road. You could have killed us. And then you start shouting your head off at me. What did you call me? Sick? A pervert? Wanting it all again the same. That I have no imagination. That I'm too scared to imagine it different.

Then you drive off and leave me in the middle of nowhere, I said.

You're lucky I even came back here. Is that what you think of me, then?

We were talking about paradise. Paradise, I shouted at the top of my voice.

I know that.

Anything you could imagine. Absolutely anything is permitted. And what do you say? That wouldn't be so bad.

She got up from the chair and shuffled across the room to the table where she rolled up her loose sleeves and set about lighting some candles set in a piece of carved driftwood. My eyes began to droop with weariness; I collapsed into the chair and watched her open some wine . . . She poured only one glass. The candle flames lashed at her in unison, and up at the wagon wheel with its miniature lampshades at the end of each spoke, at the hatchet stuck in the back of the door.

I tried to remember what had happened the night before, why she had plunged the hatchet into the door, but the thought of any other point in time, the night gone or the one to come, beyond that spectral and desolate moment as Lorna stood barely in the grasp of the candlelight at the window where the stars itched – the idea of yesterday or any other day was torturous to the point of madness. She was hoping I would go to her and put my arms round her; I knew that. She wrapped her arms around herself, still holding her glass. I wanted to burst out of myself.

167

What are we doing here? she sighed, and pressed her head against the window.

Lorna, I moaned, as though it was my last gasp, we have to go out. We can't stay in here all night again. We can't – we have to.

It was beautiful there.

Lorna, listen to me.

You know it was as well. The light and the hills. That stillness. Beautiful; there's no other word . . . But you'll never admit to it, will you? The simple beauty of it. Maybe that's what I meant, maybe I was thinking about that when I said it wouldn't be so bad.

Using both hands, she brought the glass to her mouth and sipped some wine, and that reminded me of the night at the wake while they were taking her out to bandage her hand, and how her eyes had filled over with a dirty, plaintive guiltiness. Wasn't it me who had deliberately hurt her by breaking the glass? Shouldn't it have been me feeling sorry? By constantly blaming herself, she pushed me deeper into cruelty. The doves I sent out brought back twigs of her hair.

I couldn't bear any more; I jumped out of the chair, shouting whatever came into my head (perhaps I was simply searching for a way to destroy the sorrow and the anguish that was paralysing us in that cottage)

No, it's not good enough. Beauty is no excuse. The hints and touches. The shared beauty. The just-so-ness of everything . . . the now-and-fuckenagain-ness. It's nowhere near enough. It doesn't make up for the suffering and the evil. Only a jaded priest's appetite would be satisfied by –

You don't understand me, Lorna said with scathing coldness.

I pulled the hatchet out of the door: You had this in your hand last night. Do you remember it? It's the same hatchet. Do you remember it, Lorna? Was it beautiful? You were hysterical, weren't you? Did you feel beautiful? Did you know the look you had on your face? You'd never look in the mirror again.

Shut up, she screamed at me.

And you were happy, Lorna . . . the happiest I've ever seen you.

What would you know?

You were happy, I chanted over and over again, dancing around the room, the hatchet hoisted over my head. Even at the time, I knew I was talking nonsense, spitting words out for the sake of hurting her.

She flung her glass at me and it hit the door and smashed. What's wrong with us? she shrieked, covering her face. Why can't we just be normal or something? Why do we have to do this all the time?

This brought me to my senses somehow and I dropped the hatchet on the floor; absurdly, I wished desperately for it to disappear before my eyes, for the darkness to consume it there and then. The sound of Lorna snivelling jolted me back into the room. I rushed towards her, as though propelled, then stopped, clueless to what was happening.

It's me, I heard her say. It is. I know it is.

No.

I'm so scared, she said. Niall, can we go back? Now?

I began to plead with her to stay another night. There is little sense in what I did. I was afraid of being alone, of the drive back in the dark, her abysmal sadness, of having nothing to say. One more night; I promised her everything would be fine, we would have a drink and calm down. I believed what I said. For the first time, her anguish made me afraid of her, and for her.

2

The two filthy servile salivating old men went back to their stools at the bar, leering and giggling – they leered at everything in front of their eyes. The young barman stared fondly at their shrivelled red faces and straightened his tie. I wanted him to meet my eye. Lorna was flushed like a woman who

169

has just been flattered; I sweated with the effort of controlling my anger.

I had to speak or I would crack up: You don't give a damn about them. Stop pretending you're interested in what they've got to say. Look at them. They ooze filth and ugliness. That's the real reason you want them near you, isn't it? Not politics.

I was forced to say this all in a low voice, and without moving my body. There was another man on a stool by the empty fireplace with his hands poised on his knees and a strained eye on us.

I went on: As if you gave a damn about them. Asking them about politics . . . you make me sicker than they do. Why are they so ugly? Isn't there something right and perfect about them being here? They're smirking and winking at me and talking to you about a ceasefire at the same time.

They're going to read my palm. Lorna taunted my anger with frivolity.

She finished her drink and stood up to go to the bar which was streaked with the marks of toecaps and knees like old blasts of piss on a corner wall. Her hair was limp and tangled and blacker than ever; she was noticeably pale from lack of sleep and worse. As she went towards the bar, I couldn't take my eyes off her big shoulders and the burden of her graceless hips under her long skirt. A tiny worm-eaten door behind the counter had four huge bolts on it. I had been sitting there for more than an hour listening to her and the two malignant drunks.

They're giggling at us like children, I could hardly wait to say when she sat down again with two more whiskeys. You can let them smirk at you if you want, but not at me. I was talking to you before they came over, wasn't I? They stink of piss and years-old semen. You don't even give a damn about politics – you only got into it when your true love dumped you.

I said that to incite her. At the same time, the man by the fireplace began to cough and leaned towards the grate but the phlegm stayed in his chest and he thumped at himself roughly.

170

You are a low-life bastard, Lorna whispered to me, still with that enchanted smile on her face, her lips redder than usual. If only you knew how wrong you are. About everything. I thought you –

Well then, tell me, I took both her hands. I'm as scared as you are. I need to talk tonight, Lorna. I can't cope with any more silence . . . not tonight. I was telling you about Valeria, wasn't I? And Spain and Italy. You're not even interested –

You've told me all that before. About travelling round Spain. Drifting. Begging. For absolutely no reason. Letting yourself fall. And that poor Spanish boy and the knife . . . and that girl with the white horse in the hills . . . and the time in Prague you can't remember a thing about . . . and then that other one, the mad, rich one – on the run from hope, wasn't that what you said?

You couldn't possibly understand her.

And who else was there? Some English punk and a girl from Norway who lived in caves . . . and some other girl, and then another one who you followed to Italy, jumping trains and stealing, and you had to have sex with her every time she saw a building site or a crane . . . and she vanished into air or something and –

You don't believe a word of this, do you?

And then Rome. You were so worn out you couldn't even beg anymore for scraps. And the boy prostitutes.

You like that bit, don't you? The suffering and –

But let's not forget the big miracle. Along comes Valeria – Saint Valeria who saved you from the gutter. All elegance and sophistication. You prayed one night for help on the Spanish Steps – the first words you had spoken in weeks. And the next day, lo and behold, there's Valeria. Her skin the colour of –

Darker than her large brown unblinking eyes. Yes, and I left her because she was fresh and harmless and loving. She forgave everything I did. Is that cruel enough for you? You're sick with resentment.

What do you want me to say? Lorna quickly changed tack.

Am I not telling it right? It makes me sick, do you hear me? Overindulgence and self-perpetuating despair. Is that what you left Ireland for? Freedom, do you call it? Is that all an artist can come up with these days? Sheer waste. No wonder you can't write – You're no artist.

I've wasted nothing.

You can't write.

It's a relief, I told her.

The look on her face told me she wanted to believe I was lying but couldn't.

You're too afraid to see it, she said, unconvinced.

The two old drunks were standing by our table, drooling and agitated. One of them winked at me; his lips were black; he was wearing a dirty suit jacket and another suit jacket underneath. Both of them rubbed their palms on their trousers, looking from me to Lorna with twitching, ogling eyes. They both nodded complacently when I told them to get lost.

Don't pay him any attention, Lorna said, offering them her hand.

These young ones don't know how to treat a lady, one of them jerked with laughter. His bald head was covered with scabs.

I went to the bar to get away from the sight of them. The barman had been replaced with an old woman in her house-slippers who muttered incessantly to herself out of the corners of her whiskered mouth. They were reading Lorna's palm, stroking it, sucking their gums – I kept having to turn round to observe. The coughing man was emptying his pockets on the table. Lorna laughed with them, her barren, unsavoury laugh. The bald one winked at me, as though I was playing my part properly.

I went out, to calm myself, and with some notion that being alone was better than witnessing whatever was happening inside. I wondered if I had become profoundly unbalanced and everyone but me was innocently enjoying themselves. The night air carried the scent of seaweed and dung. I took off into the darkness, only to stop after a few steps – it was suddenly unthinkable that I would survive the rest of the night by myself. Was I actually dead already as I had thought in the car? I was on the only road to the cottage but I began to worry all the same that I was bound to get lost. Valeria's eyes came into my mind at that moment, as they often did when I was profoundly afraid – the amazed, idolatrous gape with which she opened her eyes every morning on the pillow next to me, and which inspired a ferocious jealousy.

My mind was completely disordered; the horror behind me in the pub, the dark country road, Valeria's eyes, gorged with love – my thoughts crowded round me like shadows out of the trees and blocked me on all sides. Then I heard the voices of children . . .

I ran back towards the door of the pub and straight in, choking and petrified. Lorna was now holding the hand of one of the drunks – she cradled the scrawny paw in both her own hands, against her breast. The man was dancing excitedly from one foot to other like a child who needs the toilet. His nails were long and blackened. He glanced at me with blinking, startled, mingy eyes.

You must have had such a hard life, Lorna sighed heavily.

All the haggardness was gone from her face. Unkempt and glowing, I had never seen her look so beautiful. Her two lips were like gentle soothing waves closing over the head of a drowning man. My blood roared at the solitude of her dark eyes. Why did she want to disgrace herself? Was she doing it to revolt me? I stood in the door like a man stopped dead before a low, hideous vision. Lorna never once acknowledged my presence. She pressed the palsied hand deeper into her breasts.

3

I pulled out of her and came against the black silk lining of her coat which she was still wearing. We had slipped from the chair down to the floor. Her face and breasts were red and scratched from my stubble. Drinking wine, I had fallen asleep waiting on her to return to the cottage from the pub. When I woke up, most of the candles had burned out – without a second thought, I rushed across the room and started to unbutton her shirt – she was asleep in the chair. I didn't understand my own desires. Her eyes were empty, like those of someone who has been watching and waiting for a long time . . . she struggled weakly with me for a few seconds before she deserted her body and went limp under me.

Afterwards, I felt even more impatient and harassed by my own thoughts. Lorna lifted herself back into the chair and went to sleep without rearranging her clothes; one of her breasts slumped into the shadows as she slept. I decided to carry on drinking the rest of the wine, which I took outside with me when the last twitching flame and Lorna's wheezing became unbearable. I couldn't think or find any enjoyment in the night – the misty rags of mournful glory over the hills, the broken back of an old shed, the fields around me, rotten and cobwebbed. Now and again, the wind plucked at the bushes and the long grass like a lovesick lunatic at a perimeter fence.

At the sound of a scream, I ran back inside. (I remember I was grateful for the interruption.) The two old drunks were there, fondling and singing to Lorna, who was lashing at them with her arms. Hitting one with the bottle I had in my hand, I took the hatchet out of the door and started to swing it at the other one . . . he clasped his hands together and moaned some gibberish at me. I started shouting at them to get out or I'd kill them; Lorna was shouting also, pushing her breasts back inside her bra. As the bald one got up off the floor, holding his head, I gave him a kick towards the door and, while I was distracted, the other one sneaked his way quickly round the other side of me . . . I chased after them out the front door but they had already vanished. Drunk to an extreme with all the commotion, a mire of darkness on all sides of me, I cursed the two cowering stinking cretins at the top of my voice, then the night itself, and everything dreaming and lurking and sniffing in it, then my own life and the delusions that had brought me there, until I retched on my own tears, attacking the ground in a frenzy with the hatchet.

Lorna was in the cottage, huddled near the window. The last candle had gone out. Still reeling with anger, I leaned against the table, hoping she would come to comfort me; she was weeping also, I realized. I threw myself across the room in her direction, my arms outspread as though I was falling.

I shouldn't have left you alone, I apologized, purely for the relief of it.

On my knees I laid my head in her lap, my arms around her waist. She was shivering; she didn't touch me.

Then she said bleakly: I'm sorry.

What for? You did nothing.

I shouldn't have let you.

I was on the verge of killing them.

You know what I mean, she snapped.

Looking up into her face, I could see nothing. A voice in me warned that if my desolation joined with hers, we would both be wiped out. I held on tighter to her.

I thought that's what you wanted, I heard her say.

I don't understand, Lorna.

I'm sorry, she said again. Suddenly, with her legs, she pushed me backwards onto the floor.

I feel sick at myself, she began to wail. I should have stopped you – but I thought no, that's what he wants, that's what he likes. With them there watching. Why couldn't you have just stayed asleep? I can't do that sort of stuff. I just can't.

It dawned on me what she was saying. I was staggered, but not yet revolted; they had been watching from the corner while I fucked her on the floor, rubbing frantically at their hoary groins.

I'm sorry, I'm so drunk, she said.

You brought them back here for them to . . . I couldn't finish my own thought. I quelled the desire to laugh.

175

I don't know, Niall. I don't remember. I'm so drunk I think I'm going to die.

Lorna panted and choked. It was impossible to imagine so many tears, and so much snot from her nose. Her hair was wet, and her dress as far down as her belly. She must have wept for more than hour before I managed to calm her down and get her to try to sleep. Clutching my hand, she made me promise not to leave the room. I was too exhausted to be astonished or amused by what she had put herself through in an effort to please me.

Dawn – there was some kind of hollow, vitiated light in the room. Lorna was hunched on a stool near the door, wrapped in a blanket, her back to me. Waking up, I immediately noticed that I had an erection.

Lorna? Did you have another dream?

No answer.

Are you cold? Are you OK? Don't worry about anything. I feel in a bloody great mood. I've got this glimmer in me of something.

I stopped myself from going on talking; I wanted to launch into another story about myself. I could have talked about anything, about God, politics, the deserts and the seas, children, the servitude to love and sleep. Warm intoxicating doses of elation gave me thrill after thrill. As I drifted on the edge of sleep, I was engrossed by a fervent but harmonious joy somewhere deep inside me. My heart beat gladly, as strong as any world, any erection.

4

She didn't know the names of the birds, an assortment of small birds, picking through the gravel at the front door. A speckled brown one with a black beak shook the dew from its tiny splayed feathers. The early sun was out but not high enough to brighten the bare hilltops; it warmed her face and her hair, which she hadn't combed since leaving Derry. Amongst the gravel she noticed the smashed-up shell of a snail. The birds hopped and preened, their colours disappearing in flight. In a field over the road, she studied the wreck of a car overgrown with weeds, and wondered at the story behind it, and then took her eyes away suddenly as if she had been told to mind her own business. Farther off, on the crest of a biggest bare hill, she saw the burial mound; some Celtic goddess with her warriors, buried standing up, their weapons in their hands, waiting for the call to awaken and fight for the final time – that's what he had told her when they had walked up there on the afternoon of their arrival, two days before.

He had grown annoyed with her for walking so slowly, and charged on ahead. When she reached the top of the hill, he was sitting on top of a high mound of the loose stones. He said you were supposed to add your own stone every visit. She was dying of thirst; she couldn't speak. He shouted down for her to climb up to join him, kissing his fingers to show her that the view was amazing. Before she knew what she was doing, she shook her head at him in refusal, and a sadness entered her heart, a weariness with herself. What was it she was trying to deny him? Why did her anger always come back to hurt only herself? Walking around the base of the mound, she saw the sea.

He was sleeping now. Curled up in a chair, he was holding a wine bottle. Towards dawn, he must have woken up and tried to speak to her but she was too afraid to turn round in case it was a trick and somebody else was there, with a knife to his throat, forcing him to get her attention, or a gun to his head. She thought his voice had sounded strange, not frightened, careful, with a higher pitch like he was about to make a joke. As long as she didn't look, nothing could happen.

In her dream, she was waiting at the big window of a country house, maybe a castle, and everyone kept sneaking into the room to hug her, with tears of joy in their eyes, smiling and winking and kissing her; they all said, it won't be long now, I'm so happy for you. There was a big party in another room. Everyone was dressed up. They all reminded her not to waste her time staring through the window. A path of clean white gravel cut across the lawns to the door; she could see it turning into a river of tiny immaculate skulls; she could hear footsteps on the gravel . . .

Lorna began the walk along the country road to the village, a few shops and pubs and giant stones, feeling depressed and preoccupied by the awkwardness and futility of her body, the way her arms hung straight down at her side when she walked, the noise of her heavy boots on the road, the whole pointless, sagging weight of herself. The sunshine trapped in the dripping cobwebbed ditches filled her with lassitude. Even the thought of the night before, and what she had been doing with those two creepy old men, left her cold, like it was a predictable story she had heard about somebody else. All the urgency and nagging alarm of the past few months seemed to have suddenly lifted from her; she was calm and spiritless. Superstitiously, she warned herself as usual to beware of dwelling too much on herself, of allowing her own troubles to grow out of proportion, when there were people all over the world helpless, starving and forgotten.

The sea failed to clear her head, although it roared and danced and implored her to lose herself in some action beyond justice and beauty. She was attracted towards the sea wall, a barricade of enormous brand-new boulders; she sat down in the shadow of a rock, out of reach of the sun and wind. Something was different this morning, she told herself again. It was like a sense of deliverance from an unwelcome responsibility. The beach was deserted and smooth as silk and brighter than the water. Seagulls flocked and squealed around the remains of an old stone pier. She thought about Phil, about the time after he had left for London, the dreams – why hadn't she been able to go with him?

Giving up, she moved down to the sand, the sun like a slow silent explosion behind her, driving her into the sea. She gazed across the unsettled water at a fishing boat on the horizon, bemused at her own conviction that her life would have been the same no matter what choices she had made. She could hear Niall accusing her of evading the task of freedom, as he would pretentiously call it, but she knew Niall was a hypocrite, who was driven by disappointment and anger at the world, and perhaps at the very existence of the world. She smiled sadly at the thought that he might never realize he was not the hedonist he wanted to be.

She began to drift along the shore, towards the high white dunes. She stifled a sudden urge to cry. Everything was changed this morning. The sand knew the shape of her footprints, the hills knew their own reflection in the water, her breasts knew the meaning of the wall of scrubbed boulders, the wind knew the precise length of her hair. She looked around at a world drained of solitude and felt numb and ugly. She couldn't carry the burden of herself any further. Dropping to her knees, she buried her hands as far as they would go in the sand.

5

I found her, a few hours later, tramping blindly along the beach in the hot light. I was glad to see her; she didn't resist when I put my arms around her, but my heart seized up with fear and anger at her impassivity. She was colossal, and absolutely cold. In defiance, I kissed her roughly, doing my best to hide my aversion. Eventually, she pushed me away with a sterile sham of a smile and went on ahead of me, dragging her feet across the sand, her hands pushed deep into her pockets. All about us, the sea made promises it could never keep.

Later, towards midday, we were sitting together on the sand; I couldn't stop talking that morning. We watched the tide going out. I must have thought there was nothing that couldn't be said, my heart and tongue burning with a gratuitous vehemence. The seaweed along the water's edge made me think of the discarded clothes of an entire ecstatic community who had run hand in hand into the sea the night before. I said this to Lorna.

No shipwreck? You're in good form, she observed diffi-dently. It was the first time she had spoken in hours.

I'm in a great mood. I've been full of enthusiasm about something all morning – there's no call for it but I am. Empty-handed exhilaration. Maybe it's just my hangover.

My first thought that morning when I walked out of the cottage into the sunshine and the road was that the world was forgiven – but that forgiveness was no longer enough. I looked eagerly for proof in the fields and the shadows moving across the hills.

We could do anything. Steal a boat and sail away.

Don't let me stop you.

You're just scared. Don't you feel free sitting here? Come on, let's just forget about last night. We were both off our heads.

I've nothing left, Lorna vowed, with a raised, fraught voice. Then she regained control of herself: I feel like I'm a ghost, less than a ghost. Still . . . very, very still. Tranquil. I'm not fighting any more, Niall. I'm not even afraid any more.

We should go away. I'm dead serious, Lorna.

I had not put any thought into this idea.

Lorna laughed painfully and threw a handful of sand into the air. Farther up the beach, I noticed what looked like dogs running in and out of the water, big long-haired animals, tangling with each other and bolting suddenly towards the open sea.

We could, Lorna. What's keeping us here? Nothing. What's there to stop us? We can do whatever we –

Will you do me a favour and stop pretending that you want something more out of this other than –

Other than what?

I don't want to fight, Niall. I don't care any more.

That's a lie, I accused her, moving up onto my knees. That's not what's stopping you from going. You've some warped idea that it's a sin or something to run away.

I had my chance, she said pathetically.

That's ridiculous. What are you talking about?

She shouted at me: We've no right to be sitting here.

Now it was me who laughed in derision. Right?

We've no right, she repeated prudishly.

I thumped the sand in protest. She made no sense to me in that state of mind, sitting cross-legged in her big overcoat. There was sand in her hair, under the rings on her fingers, filling the eyelets of her boots. I stared at the side of her fleshy, purgative face and imagined the bronzed domes and belfries of a vague sultry city behind her, instead of the old florid lies of the sea.

Then she told me about what had been going through her mind that morning before I showed up. She spoke in a deadened voice, without moving her head, staring out at the water, perhaps at the tanker, or the long clouds on the horizon, or the distant waves in the sunshine, single tears running down her face and dropping into her lap. She talked about her nightmares, about Phil who had left her to go to London and the night she packed her bags to follow him; she sat in the hall but felt paralysed when the taxi horn sounded in the street, and the driver banged on the door and cursed. She sat there for hours until the silence in the street began to frighten her and she had the terrible thought that everyone had been evacuated except her. She opened the door and found a drunk asleep on her step . . . she took him inside.

She wouldn't say any more. I goaded her with my incomprehension of what she wanted to say by telling me this. She took a stone out of her pocket; I recognized it as the chunk of speckled marble I had left on the burial mound. Forcing another mocking smile, she put it into my hand.

Is this just about another dream? You're not making any sense, you know, Lorna.

The dogs were barking. She wanted me to believe that she had reached a final, absurd, zealous resignation.

I'm dead on my feet, she said, And you're talking about sightseeing. I don't even know how I'm supposed to keep going, teaching, paying the rent, people, protesting – I don't want to see you any more, Niall.

I said nothing. I felt instantly alone.

Do you hear me, Niall? It's not right.

I persisted with my silence. She wanted me to argue with her – she hoped I would try to dissuade her from leaving me. I know now that this wasn't true. Leaning back, I threw the stone she had given me as far as I could towards the receding tide. One of the dogs went after it, and almost caught it before the stone landed in the wet sand . . . the dog then bounded straight for us up the beach, with wide empty eyes, veering off only at the last moment when Lorna and I both raised our hands to defend ourselves.

I started to laugh. Lorna unfolded her legs and clumsily got to her feet into the force of the wind. Holding on to her hair, she said: I'm sorry. It grated on me to think that she was worried about hurting me. I'm sorry, she said again. She wrapped her coat around her and headed off along the beach. I watched her, recording in my mind her heavy gait across the strand, the gulls, the way the sea seemed to have gone out only in the middle of the beach, the polished boom of rocks in the distance, and then the two long-haired dogs, biting playfully at each other, who ran after her.

I saw them leap on her together; their front legs caught her squarely in the back, knocking her face down in the sand. The dogs ran on as though nothing had happened, and doubled back suddenly, galloping past me towards two women further along the beach, who were waving their arms and calling. The dark shape of Lorna lay motionless on the sand. It didn't occur to me to run and help her.

After too long a time, I saw her begin to move. She managed to get to her knees. The two dog-owners were hurrying in the other direction. With her head bowed, as if she was praying in the wind, Lorna stayed on her knees; I still had no thought of going to her. She turned towards me then. Her face and hair were plastered with sand. A deep ache started in me as I tried to meet her gaze, a pity that was suffocating and maddening. Privately I begged her to smile or give some sign that she knew this was merely an absurd accident, two dogs getting carried away on the beach and knocking her off balance.

She gave me that look of apology then. The pity in me turned to horror and outrage – at the sight of her lewd remorse, I wanted to shout at her, to slap her face. Without brushing the sand off her face, she stood up and resumed her track across the beach, her arms hanging limply by her sides, past the sea wall, until she disappeared amongst the dunes. Appalled, I sat there on that beach for hours. The day grew colder, dim and unsettled.

6

I met Martina on the street as I was coming out of the old people's home. She had Louise with her, in her school uniform. I felt embarrassed at meeting them, as if I had been caught red-handed at the scene of a crime. To my surprise, Martina threw her arms around me. She was crying. At the sight of her mother weeping, Louise began to cry also, helplessly, without trying to wipe the tears away. What else could I do but laugh, confronted by their wet, gasping faces? Soon enough, Louise joined in, laughing as loud as she could, bending over and slapping her white knee. Martina then made out that she was offended by our hilarity and walked away across the car park with her nose in the air. Louise choked so much she lost her breath and her face turned crimson, the ends of her hair sucked into her mouth. I pointed to an old man waving from one of the windows. This was shortly after Lorna was buried.

A male nurse with tattooed arms had led me through the corridors (the place seemed clean and bright but I was bewildered by the noise coming from each of the rooms, which seemed full of people talking and moving furniture and eating) and outside to a tarmacked courtyard, where he pointed at my mother in her wheelchair and then slowly pulled the trigger of his imaginary pistol and blew on the smoking barrel. In the sunshine, my mother unsteadily raised one of her bare hefty arms and took aim back. The nurse ducked behind me with the cry: You wouldn't shoot your own son, would you, Maureen O'Kelly?

She opened fire four times, making farting sounds with her lips. She was wearing a torn straw hat and gangster sunglasses. Squeezed into the wheelchair, her body was unrecognizable and shapeless, and her head had grown to an abnormal size – blunted and cumbrous as a cow's head. A nurse sat on a stood beside her, sunbathing, the white skirt pulled up over knees, white clogs.

What's he want? My mother jerked her head towards me when I sat down on a stool beside them.

The nurse leaned towards her and shouted into her ear that I had come to arrest her. My mother shook with silent laughter.

It's your own son there, Maureen, will you catch yourself on.

Scowling, my mother shifted her weight in the chair and reached down to the fire bucket between them. The nurse jumped to her feet.

If you throw one more bit of sand at me, Maureen, I'll fucken lock you in a room and throw away the key. Do you hear me?

Who do you think you're codding? My mother grimaced and patted her hat clumsily down on her head.

The nurse turned to me: She's just letting on, you know. I don't care what the fucken doctors say. Tell her your name. Go on. Shout it at her. Though she's probably letting on to be deaf as well. O'Kelly, I said, acutely embarrassed. I was unable to shout. My mother was looking the other way.

Did you hear that Maureen? He said his name was O'Kelly. It's your bloody son. Come on, catch yourself on.

In another corner of the courtyard, motionless, his head slightly bowed, an old bald man in a baggy suit and tie was holding a basin out under the sky: the expression on his face indicated that he dreaded to think what he was going to catch in it.

We had to cut the wedding ring off her the other day, the

nurse told me in a softer voice while we both stared at my mother, who seemed to be gazing up at the sun. A man came over from the hospital. We were all geared up for a big fight. But she was as quiet as a mouse. Not a word out of her. She wanted an envelope to put the pieces in. Like two wee gold eyelashes. Then she starts going on about a stamp. But she's no idea where she wants to send it.

My mother slapped the arm of the wheelchair with her swollen fingers. Sure I know the O'Kellys. Nancy O'Kelly from Stanley's Walk. Sure didn't she marry Polo Barney from The Lone Moor? That son of theirs who was shot. And his wee girl high up in Tillys. Am I right or not?

She turned towards me: Am I right or not?

I stuttered and shrugged my shoulders.

Away you and get lost, she sneered at me.

The nurse threw up her arms in despair: So who are you then, Maureen? Your name's fucken O'Kelly too, isn't it ? Excuse my bad mouth.

My mother had a great laugh at that. The dark glasses fell lopsided under the broken straw brim. She even tried to elbow me to join in with the joke. Then her temper flared all of a sudden:

You'd be more on your bloody line getting that fella a cup of tea or something while he's waiting for his mother. I know your type all right. You took my family allowance book from under my pillow, didn't you? I see right through, so I do. That man in the Credit Union is coming in to see me the day so I want my hair done.

The nurse had already sat back on the stool; she shut her eyes and began to hum to herself.

My mother pulled off her straw hat and threw it into the courtyard towards the old man with the basin in his outstretched hands.

Martina persuaded me to come back to their house with them, assuring me that Michael wouldn't be back until late. She said that I looked like I could do with a proper meal. We took a black taxi from the Strand Road; Martina talked to the driver, whose wife she knew; I listened while Louise read to me proudly from one of her school books, screwing her finger tightly into each word, traces of glitter in the clear varnish on her nails.

Without taking off her coat, Martina set about peeling some spuds for a stew as soon as we got into the house. We gave Louise all of our attention, knowing that we would have to wait until she was in bed before we would be faced with the business of talking to each other. There was a powerful sense of relief in this postponement, a giddy awareness of how easily everything can be forgotten, and for a few hours the three of us played and joked and told stories as though we were amazed at how simple and precious and sudden this time was.

After we had eaten, coaxed by her mother, Louise stood in the middle of the kitchen and sang a song. Her hair was wrecked and the line of her mouth was caked with stew. Clasping her hands behind her back, already out of breath, she sang in a thin, tangled voice to the fluorescent light in the ceiling. It was a song about the sea, a mermaid. Martina had to help her with the words at one point but Louise carried on untroubled, her face reddening and growing more glazed and incredulous until she seemed to have forgotten where she was and what she was doing, staring beyond us, beguiled into a guiltless rapture of shingle and golden scales – it was watching her that I began to grieve over Lorna's death for the first time.

The song finished, Louise curtsied and I stared at her, powerless to move. My chest heaved and ached as if I was sobbing but my breathing seemed to have stopped. Martina was applauding, her glances urging me, then pleading with me, to show her daughter some appreciation. I had the horrible sensation of being trapped in a photograph – a picture of a man frozen on the brink of moral paralysis. Clapping my hands, even forming a smile for Louise, seemed as big a task as killing somebody. I thought I could see Lorna in one of the chairs, sticking welts of her hair into the bullet holes in her head and chest, sucking the bloodied ends with pleasure and jabbering to herself: copulating in the foam . . . copulating in the foam. Suddenly, Louise wailed with fear; she ran to her mother who was examining my face with appalling disbelief.

Eventually, Martina pulled Louise out of the room as if she saving her from the sight of me. Left alone, I was afraid of myself, and everything around me. The table and chairs, the plates, a sauce bottle and a vase, crumbs on the plastic table-cloth, my shadow – they all seemed to have been dumped away in a back room, useless, garish, slapstick. A teaspoon lying on the table, glued on like a stage prop, made me sick to the pit of my stomach. Upstairs, I could hear Martina and Louise moving about, the child's whining confusion, Martina losing her temper.

Lorna's death was like something looming at the window, the back door, surrounding the house, trying to find a way in. Sniggering at what would happen when the walls gave way, she danced around the kitchen in a white hospital gown or she changed costume and stepped into a memory, arguing politics with people in a crowded pub, in the rain on the street walking sullenly with her arms folded under her breasts in a long black coat, and lying naked and cold and flaccid under me in a darkened room embittered with the smoke of joss sticks.

I didn't wait for Martina to come back down: I dreaded the silence that would follow after she had stopped reading to Louise, the footstep on the top stair, the riven, trembling way she would collect the dishes and tidy up without looking at me. I knew I had done an irrevocable wrong. Convincing myself that it would be a further insult to her to believe an explanation or an apology would have any worth, I told myself to get out of there as quickly as possible. With my eyes closed, I made it to the street. It was dark. The street was quiet, unfinished, mounds of shining sand lit up at the hinterland. Wrapped in plastic, a bus stop sign lay along a garden wall. I stumbled along, exhausted by myself, thinking of nothing more than the journey back to the flat, stretched out on my bed in the darkness, the stamina I needed to reach there. At the main road, a car passed me . . .

It skidded into a turn, accelerated and came back in my direction. A glance over my shoulder told me somehow the car was heading straight for me. I should have run towards the lighted windows of a factory up ahead – one of those American companies Lorna railed against because they would not allow the workers to be part of a union. The speeding headlights offered me a luminous abyss of remorse to fall back into. Perhaps because I was practically drunk with weariness, I had the same feeling of elation as that night when the police had caught me in the grounds of the old people's home. I stopped, stood still, savouring the excitement, the unanswerable judgement about to be placed on my head.

Fucken say one for me as well while you're at it.

The car had stopped beside me, the door had opened. I heard my brother's voice.

I bet your shambles of a life couldn't even be bothered to flash before you. Get in the car.

We drove in towards the city centre, past the school playing fields, the ghostly totems of tall skeletal H's in the gloom. We went on past the shops at Pennyburn. Seeing that we were not taking the quickest route to my place, I imagined that he was driving me out into the countryside to have his final say, maybe dump me there naked with a bag over my head.

Don't blame Martina. It was me. I asked her if I could come down to the house. Her and Louise were outside the home when I came out.

I was handing him an opportunity to attack me. We were waiting in a line of traffic at the army barracks. The high green gate was sliding open to let in a foot patrol. One of the soldiers made a theatrical bow to the cars and ran inside. Michael hit his horn and a few other cars joined in, a comical medley of horns. The red tabernacle eyes gleamed at the invisible peak of the surveillance tower

I'm sorry about that girl, the shooting. It makes a mockery of everything. When . . .

Michael blew out his cheeks and pushed the glasses back up his nose. He was letting me know that he had talked to Martina. Or perhaps Danny had told him something at my Da's grave.

You didn't know her – I said this in a giddy tone that made the words unintelligible.

He rolled down his window. A group of teenagers were drinking at the corner of a street.

Was she a teacher?

She was a socialist.

He raised his thin eyebrows. Aren't we all?

Do you think so?

He didn't answer.

She had this question . . . about whether or not you would release a gas into the world that would take away all suffering. Whether you press the button or not.

I'll have to ask Ma that one, he said dryly.

She'd say do it.

Would she now?

At one time she would have.

Well there's your answer then. You grow up. Wise up.

Kneel down, you mean.

You're the only one I see on their knees. He sounded pleased with this retort. As he turned the car into my street, he glanced at me in search of some question but I let him think he had silenced me. Pulling in outside my flat, he turned off the engine. He looked up at my building and asked me a few questions about the place, whether it was warm, the neighbours, the rent.

That girl's death wasn't your fault. He turned towards me suddenly in the seat and took off his glasses. I know what you're like. Do you hear me?

Instead of making me laugh, this notion depressed me.

Do you hear me? Don't fall into that trap. You got out, so stay out.

Out where? I get this feeling I haven't been anywhere . . . All that shite about travel broadening the mind.

Listen to yourself, will you? Don't come yamming back here like the prodigal son. This city isn't your own private confession box. People have enough to be getting on with without your type beating their breasts about leaving all around the streets.

I don't know where to go, I told him honestly.

I don't give a shite. Get yourself out of here. That girl's dead. Just move on. Pronto.

In a flash of anger I said: Or I'll end up like you?

He grabbed hold of me by the neck. His eyes, struggling to retain their anger, shifted from my stubborn face to my hands that did nothing to protect myself, to the street where a man and a woman walked arm in arm under a streetlight pretending not to have noticed us. His grip loosened, tightened again briefly, but he failed to find the words he wanted. As he let go of me he pulled on the car door and swung it open.

I'm sorry, Michael. What else do you want me to say?

There's plenty.

He drove off while I was still standing in the road. I knew he would be cursing himself for having lost his temper. He would sit up late that night by the kitchen window feeling he had failed in his obligations as my older brother, trying to quell the anger at the heart of his sense of duty towards that stringent, lying, murky, nail-bitten city.

7

It was a Saturday morning and a group of teenagers were sitting on a garden wall across the street. They looked at their hands or spat between their feet or scathingly squinted into a distance they already knew didn't exist – four boys and two girls. None of them bothered to glance up at the sound of a helicopter. I left the window and searched under my bed for some papers. When I came back to my chair, after only a few minutes, the wall was empty and the pavement was mottled with spit.

I forced my attention back to the story I was writing. A little later, two of the Spanish students left the building hand in hand. I said to myself that I had to make some effort to get to know them; the week before, one of the boys had knocked on my door to invite me to a party that I had forgotten about. He then had the nerve to ask me if I knew where he could buy some dope. The cars that passed were mainly occupied by mothers and fathers going to do their week's shopping at the big supermarkets.

This was about three weeks after the day on the beach with Lorna, where she had left me to find my own way back to Derry. I had seen nothing of her since then. I usually thought about her around dusk, as the lights came on along the streets – I pictured her lying on her sofa under her tartan blanket, with the TV throwing shadows across her face and the walls. The curtains were tightly closed and a joss stick turned to a slim shell of ash in a wooden holder Jim had made for her, and there was always water running in the kitchen because she once said that the sound made it impossible to think. At dusk, I would stop work and lie on my bed.

I had started to write a novel; I was able to forget about myself for hours on end. There was no reason for the tranquillity and the sense of recuperation I was feeling. The days were long and indistinct but the loneliness was tolerable. Generally, I went out for last orders in the pubs. The thought nagged at me that I would have to pay a price for this beneficence; I blamed Lorna for creating this superstition in me. Very late one night I woke with a poem in my mouth for her, but as soon as I tried to write it down I was blocked by a peculiar loathing. Every word of it was out of place, noxious, and strictly deformed. All I remember of it now is that it contained the word cholesterol.

I looked across the street at the wall again. The plaster had dropped off in places. Underneath, there was red brick, a soft, bright umber that reminded me of Italy. In the past, the concrete parapet had been drilled with holes for railings, probably to keep the kids from hanging about on it. The holes were now full of old rainwater and crisp bags. Two girls, with one hand each, pushed a pram down the street. I decided to make a cup of tea; I had to shake myself out of this idle daydreaming.

Danny knocked as I was pouring water into the cup. I wasn't expecting him; I had seen him the night before when we went for a silent walk as far as the border. At the sight of him that morning, tousled and trembling, I thought he had been in a fight. Instinctively, I glanced down at his thin white fists for traces of blood, his clothes for a sign of struggle and down at his shoes, one of which was muckier than the other. He shook his head in annoyance to all my questions, unable to speak.

Do you want me to guess? I laughed.

He glared violently at the cup in my hand, then a pile of my clothes in the corner.

Have you been sacked? Did you go ahead and tell the manager what you thought of him?

I took a step back, suddenly worried he was going to throw a punch at me. He jerked his head towards the door. I didn't understand. He tried to speak but his mouth was dried up . . . I brought him some water and held the glass to his mouth; his hands were shaking.

Is it Noreen? . . . Or Lorna?

I saw something skim across the surface of his eyes, like a bird across a roof. He crossed the room to the window and looked down at the street.

I'm doing some work, Danny. I don't –

I'm not asking. If you don't see – you won't fucken believe it, will you? Fucken . . .

His eyes were dim and ferocious as he charged across the room at me. I backed into a corner. For a brief, intoxicating moment, I saw into a type of rage that reminded me of the night in the old asylum – I wasn't afraid; I wanted to fall on my knees and worship it.

You won't fucken believe anything, will you? he raged at

me. You'll fucken see now, all right – you don't fucken believe anything.

We stared at each other; with regret, I saw the anger in his eyes (it was like watching him die) slowly sink out of sight . . . he blinked, and there was the humble fear again.

Get your coat.

I followed Danny through the town. He didn't speak a word. Feeling nervous, I started to talk about a scrap between two dogs earlier on the street; I told him I had got another letter from Valeria and that she wanted me to meet her in London. *Perché i mei sentimenti d'amore per te ti rendono così infelice?* Why does my love for you make you so unhappy? I could tell that what I was saying irritated him to the point where he couldn't endure my presence. At the time, I put it down to his own problems with Noreen. I was anticipating another day in the pub, listening to him, resenting his annoyance when I wanted to talk about my own troubles. I reminded myself that I was leaving soon anyway.

We stopped and looked up Rosseville Street at an army cordon. Two Saracens blocked off the pavements. Soldiers kneeled in shop doorways behind the tape where a small crowd had gathered, mostly beggars and winos and old women. Some bored journalists were standing around a TV van in a side street, laughing with a group of kids.

After a minute or so I expected us to move on, but Danny seemed lost in contemplation. To wake him up, I made some joke about the mental condition of most of the onlookers; one of the winos had started into a jig in the street. An old woman blessed herself.

I wonder what happened, I said then, without the least interest.

A shooting, Danny informed me. This morning. Early on.

I heard the helicopter just. Anybody hit?

One, he growled.

Another wino approached the police line and began to describe the underhandedness of everything alive and not to an RUC man.

A fucken balls-up, said Danny.

Come on. By the look of you, they'll haul you in if we stand here any longer.

I went to put my hand on his shoulder but stopped for some reason I couldn't figure out. Danny sucked in his breath and looked at the white sky above Creggan on the hill.

Two snipers. A foot patrol on the street – and who do they get?

I gave the refrain: It's one balls-up after another.

Danny put his eyes against mine – like a rioting crowd running towards me. Who do they get? he insisted.

A dog taking a piss. (I said that because a mongrel was running around with a length of police tape in its mouth.)

Who do they get?

Lay off me, Danny.

This morning? he shouted at me as though it was the time of day that mattered. Even then, I thought he was furious because the snipers had been so incompetent.

She was walking along the street by herself, he roared into my face.

I cannot account for the effect those few words had on me. A rush of cold horror knocked me off balance. I put my hand on his shoulder to steady myself; I thought I was going to be sick, or shit myself there on the street. What was it about those words that captured her? When Danny put his arm around my back, I wanted to beg him to leave me alone. I saw flashes of a smoky bird-filled sky, a wino dancing with his hands over his face, the tears on Danny's thin white lips, a three-legged dog, and the helicopter at last, swinging from one spot to another like –

She was walking along the street? I said, and I was crying now also.

Danny's grip tightened around me like he was pushing me towards the edge of a cliff.

Is she still there? I shouted, staggered by the image of Lorna lying on the street, under some stranger's coat or an old blanket, an affront to all eyes, the ends of her black hair scratching the pavement for clemency.

They took her away, Danny said. She's not there. The ambulance was on the TV, Niall.

Pushing Danny aside, I started walking towards the cordon. Two RUC men spotted me immediately; one of them lowered his chin to speak into a radio on his flak jacket. They would have seen the tears on my face by now . . . I took my hands out of my pockets and saw the helicopter swinging back and forth in the sky – like it was keeping time with the steps of the wino's intensifying dance. Out of the corner of my eye, I was aware of a soldier with his gun trained on me. I couldn't bear to know what I was going to do. Danny shouted my name. Walking straight at the cordon, I shut my eyes.

Lorna was there; she was far away from me, like a leaf caught in a gust of wind, fluttering and spinning, but I could still see the sand on her cheeks, her horseshoe frown, her left eyebrow cocked in doubt, her penitential smile. I was hurrying towards her as fast as I could but the wind flung her about – she was blown about in all directions. I thought I had something important to tell her.

She was blown into my face like an old rag.

Epilogue

The sadness in the way she undid her bra or stepped out of her knickers was proof that the world existed: her death undermined everything.

I was incapable of laying eyes on her. She faded out of sight across the white strand, sandy paw-marks on the back of her coat – that was my last image of her until she stepped shyly into my dreams.

All this seems absurd to me now. I wish I could say that I am dreaming it up for my own amusement. There is nothing to stop me forgetting. But then why do I feel I have made a deliberate shambles of telling it? Every word disgusts me, off-key and pretentious. A vague regret stirs in me when I think back to that time in Derry.

I craved an impossible ultimatum.

My life was in spate.

But I am a long way away now. In this other city, I can look through the windows into the rooms of the king's palace whenever I want to remind myself that only luxury lasts for ever. The snow taught me that forgiveness is not everything.

Lorna once said that socialism would outlive any idea of beauty. Her death was ugly and sudden and meaningless to anyone who didn't know her. Danny leaned over the coffin and kissed her lips. Perhaps it was that kiss alone that caused him to lose his mind?

He was in the back yard, hanging out clothes on the line, when the sun broke free and he saw a shadow on the back door in the shape of a woman's head. Although he told himself it was only the morning rain drying out of the wood, he was frightened and went back inside. He made a cup of tea but he never drank it. In his slippers, he walked over to Lorna's house to let her parents in on what he had seen. He came back home and asked his mother to take a look, but she could see nothing but an old stain. Over the next few weeks, Danny began to tell everyone he met, in the hotel, in bars, around the streets, about Lorna's face appearing to him on the back door. He went to the priest with his news and decided to stop an army foot patrol while he was on his way to the shops for his mother. He was painting a placard to march around with in the Guildhall Square when the doctor knocked on his bedroom door.

Danny writes that he has never felt better. He calls me a smithereen, who must now forget there was ever an explosion. Martina must have given him my address; I let her know what I am doing, now and again. He admits to me that some darker part of him was always waiting for the chance to sneak out and take him over completely; he wonders if this is the reason why he never felt safe or sure of himself anywhere outside of Derry. I want to ask him to send me a rubbing of the step where I saw the purifier.

When Lorna visits me, she seems embarrassed at her own audacity; she wants to hear my dreams.

At night, the beam from the lighthouse sweeps across my room and fills the mirrors to satiety. In the morning, they do not give back my reflection straight away.

These fragments imprison her more ruthlessly than her tortured dreams. A young woman feels her knees go from under her an instant before the finger of an unknown man bends around a shining trigger –

No. A young woman caught in a crossfire – an accident, nothing more. Life is no work of art . . . and neither are you, she used to say to me when I complained about somebody. If there had been heavy rain that day, or the wind had kept her a few seconds longer at the corner . . .

If I had loved her . . . would that be art?

I have been trying to remember her in order to chase her away. Perhaps I have tried to tell the story ineptly to avoid any insinuation of penance. Why would anyone believe that recalling this maelstrom of delusion and anguish would make me a better person? The hand of suffering is not strong enough to slap the arse of the world into being.

I listen for the first joyful squeal of hunger along the docks. Lumps of red and yellow ice float between the rusting boats and the frozen rubbish. A fog pours in – it reminds me of the happy gas Lorna believed she would never release at any cost.

This world is not waning.

The one who keeps me sane now wears a knife in her fur-lined boot. She uncovers her breasts as if she had faith in no other form of madness.